"Do you want to st
press presence die̶s̶ ̶d̶o̶

Isla knew she did not want to fight her way through a small skirmish each time she entered or left her home. And Gabe seemed really sincere. He was completely different to how she'd imagined him from reading about him in the gossip columns. And he was her employer! How much time would she have to be alone with him, really? His daughter would be there on weekends. And workdays, Isla could maybe stay in her room? Lock the door if she felt she needed to? "Thank you. I might take you up on that offer. But what about your daughter? Won't she be confused if you have some strange woman stay at yours? Or is she used to it?"

Gabe smiled and shook his head. "I've never had a strange woman stay at mine. Just nannies, or family members. No celebs. No one-night stands. I'm not that kind of guy."

"Okay. Thank you. But just for a few days. No more than that."

Dear Reader,

In this story, you get to meet Isla, a woman who has PTSD from an attack. It was something I wanted to explore, how the echoes of that incident could infiltrate into her life for many years afterward and who the right guy that might be able to help her silence those echoes could possibly be.

And in walked my gorgeous plastic surgeon, Mr. Gabriel Newton. Gabriel's job is to make people feel better about themselves, and I wanted to write a hero who did this 100 percent, without knowing how to make himself feel good.

And so, who better to help him than Isla?

I hope you will enjoy their story as they try to navigate the strange nuances of life, fate and love.

Warmest wishes,

Louisa xxx

RESISTING THE SINGLE DAD SURGEON

LOUISA HEATON

MEDICAL ROMANCE

Harlequin®
MEDICAL ROMANCE

Recycling programs for this product may not exist in your area.

ISBN-13: 978-1-335-94272-2

Resisting the Single Dad Surgeon

Copyright © 2024 by Louisa Heaton

Harlequin Enterprises ULC
22 Adelaide St. West, 41st Floor
Toronto, Ontario M5H 4E3, Canada
www.Harlequin.com

Printed in U.S.A.

Louisa Heaton lives on Hayling Island, Hampshire, with her husband, four children and a small zoo. She has worked in various roles in the health industry—most recently four years as a community first responder, answering emergency calls. When not writing, Louisa enjoys other creative pursuits, including reading, quilting and patchwork—usually instead of the things she *ought* to be doing!

Books by Louisa Heaton

Harlequin Medical Romance

Christmas North and South

A Mistletoe Marriage Reunion

Yorkshire Village Vets

Bound by Their Pregnancy Surprise

Greenbeck Village GPs

The Brooding Doc and the Single Mom
Second Chance for the Village Nurse

Night Shift in Barcelona

Their Marriage Worth Fighting For

Miracle Twins for the Midwife
Snowed In with the Children's Doctor
Single Mom's Alaskan Adventure
Finding Forever with the Firefighter

Visit the Author Profile page
at Harlequin.com for more titles.

For Faisal, Hayley and Natalie x

Praise for
Louisa Heaton

"Another enjoyable medical romance from
Louisa Heaton with the drama coming courtesy of
life on a busy maternity ward. Lovely characters, a
great story, set in one of my favourite cities and an all
round easy engaging read."
—*Goodreads* on *Miracle Twins for the Midwife*

CHAPTER ONE

THE GARLAND CLINIC was situated midway down Harley Street. Pristine. As aesthetically perfect as any old town house could possibly be, its exterior was pure white, the glossy black door framed by two thick white columns, and the path that led to the door was black and white checked, lined by ball-shaped topiaries.

A brass plaque on the door let Isla and its clients know that this wasn't any ordinary house. It might look like an old domestic setting, but inside promised to be modern. Exacting and to a high standard.

She sucked in a deep breath, placed a smile upon her face and pushed open the door, revealing a warm and welcoming entryway. A long corridor lay straight ahead, but to her left was a reception desk with staff behind it. A receptionist in a crisp white blouse and black skirt and a guy in scrubs, holding a file in one hand and a phone in the other as he chatted to someone about a reservation he had the next evening.

The receptionist looked up at Isla and smiled. 'Can I help you?'

'Miss Isla French. I'm the new surgical nurse starting today.'

'Oh, yes! We've been expecting you. Why don't you take a seat and I'll see if Mr Garland is free?'

Isla took a seat. She'd met Mr Garland, the senior partner of the clinic. He had interviewed her, alongside Mr Sharma, one of the other surgeons. There should have been a third consultant there, a Mr Newton, she believed, the one she'd seen often in Mack Desveaux's gossip magazine when she'd been researching the clinic, but he'd been called away on an emergency, so they'd not met yet.

Both consultants had seemed very nice. Approachable. Friendly. Mr Garland specialised in breast reconstructions, Mr Sharma in liposuction and tummy tucks, whereas Mr Newton specialised in faces. Facelifts, rhinoplasties, that kind of thing.

It was exactly the kind of clinic she'd been looking for. Where she could continue to be a nurse, but where all the surgeries done were *elective*, cosmetic procedures. Nothing that was life or death. Nothing that provoked strong emotions. Nothing that could put her at risk.

Finding a clinic that she could get to on the bus had also been a bonus. Finding a place so close to the friend's flat she was staying in temporarily until she could find something more permanent had been like a sign that this job posting had been made just for her, and so she'd been thrilled to receive the phone call from Mr Garland that they'd like to offer her the position of surgical nurse.

'Would you like a beverage?' the receptionist asked. 'We have tea, coffee, water, juice?'

'I'm all right, thank you.'

'I'm Jane. Might as well get to know one another, seeing as we're going to be colleagues.'

'Isla.'

'Such a lovely name!'

Isla smiled. How were you supposed to respond to that? It wasn't as if she'd chosen it herself. But she didn't have too much time to worry. She heard footsteps coming down the stairs and then there was a very handsome man standing in front of her. Mr Newton. Plastic surgeon to the stars. Hair as black as a raven's wing, slightly rakish, slightly ruffled. Bed hair, she liked to think of it, but styled perfectly. He had icy blue eyes and dark stubble, cheekbones you could cut yourself with and a strong, square jaw. He turned his gaze over the waiting room, where he saw her and paused briefly before a wide smile broke across his face. 'Miss French? Mr Gabriel Newton. I don't believe I've had the pleasure yet.'

She was aware of how she must look. Gabriel Newton was clearly a man who assessed faces for a living. He scanned them, found their faults and automatically could think of how much better they might look once graced by his scalpel or bone hammer. And despite her having tried her best this morning, she knew she did not look as beautiful as the models and movie stars he was often seen out and about with.

Her hair was tied tight to the back of her head in a bun, as she liked to keep it out of the way when she was at work. She wore the bare minimum of make-up. A little eyeliner. A little lip gloss. Some concealer to hide the dark marks under her eyes, but that was it. And she'd never had cosmetic surgery. No plumpers. No fillers. Nothing. He probably looked at her and thought of all the ways she could be improved.

But she smiled back anyway. Because she was here to work. To be a professional, not to be a model, or a muse.

'Hello. Call me Isla.' She stood and held out her hand, trying not to be mesmerised by those blue eyes of his. She could see now, in person, why the paparazzi loved him so. He was a perfect sculpture of a man. Handsome. Beautiful. No doubt photogenic. He looked daring and racy and probably helped sell more magazines than he ought to, because of the company that he kept.

'Isla. Call me Gabe.'

He shook her hand and she felt something race

up her arm. A tingle. A warmth. And then a flush of heat that suffused her face and neck.

Am I blotchy? I bet I'm blotchy.

The thought annoyed her. Irritated her. This was not what she'd wanted! She'd just wanted to return to work and get on with her day. Meet with everyone and then just be the best surgical nurse that she could be.

Not this.

Not this complication.

Putting it down to first-day nerves, she dismissed the idea that she might be even the slightest bit attracted to him and pushed the thought to one side. Because there was a danger of becoming enamoured with someone and just because they had a pretty face did not mean that they were a nice person. Danger could lurk behind even the nicest facades and she knew this to her detriment.

Gabe was gorgeous and rich, according to the gossip, but who was he really? Clever, no doubt, he was a surgeon, but beauty was superficial at best. So she could shove his good looks and her initial crush reaction into a box marked *Nothing Worth Worrying Over.* And *her* visage? Was nothing she wanted to do anything about. She'd never considered cosmetic surgery herself and so her face was her face and life was life. It had marred her with worry lines and crow's feet and dark shadows, but they told a story. They marked her as being someone who'd experienced things. Even if hardly any of them were pleasant.

So sue me if I'm not perfect.

She'd never wanted perfection. There was nothing interesting about perfection.

'Have you had the tour?' he asked.

'No.'

'Then let me show you around. It can be a bit of a maze, to begin with.' He had a dynamite smile. Lovely, straight teeth. Wide, full lips. And he smelt great. She could feel her senses going into overdrive and struggled to rein them in. As he showed her the consulting rooms, surgical rooms, recovery rooms, day ward, staffrooms, stock rooms, utilities, she kept getting wafts of his scent, flashes of his smile, and was acutely aware of his height and power.

He was a tall man. Over six feet, for sure. Broad shoulders, neat waist, his bespoke tailored suit clinging to him in ways that ought to be illegal. Gabriel Newton clearly worked out and looked after himself, but then she supposed he needed to, doing the job that he did. Gabe was a salesman. An advertising board. A look-at-what-you-could-be-too image. He had to look good. It made the clients, the patients, feel comfortable. Assured of their results. But as he showed her around, introducing her to various members of staff, she saw no obvious signs of surgery on his face. No scars. No nips. No tucks. Nothing pulled tight. He looked completely natural and she felt like looking up into the heavens and whispering, *Well done*.

'You can put your things here.' He indicated a free locker in one of the staff areas. They had a locker room, their own shower and toilet facilities. A small gym with workout equipment. A fully equipped kitchen and a lounge. It really was quite amazing!

Isla shrugged off her jacket and hung it up with her bag. She closed her locker with the key and slipped it into her pocket.

'Scrubs are in here. Freshly laundered every day. Used ones go in that hamper over there— don't ever wear them home.'

'All right.'

'Can I make you a drink?' He checked his watch. 'You've got time before your first surgery.'

'Perfect. Tea, please.'

'Coming right up.' He gave her a dazzling smile that almost knocked her off her feet and she nervously sat down on one of the sofas, not sure what to do with herself.

'Do you know what my first procedure is?'

'You're in with me. Rhinoplasty.'

Nose job. 'Okay.'

'Phil says you've worked as a surgical nurse before. In plastics?'

Phil was Phillip Garland. The boss.

'A few times. I worked in a burns unit for a while, too. We did a lot of maxillofacial surgeries, but I've mostly worked in general surgery.'

'So you have a broad knowledge base?'

'I think so. I hear you specialise in facial procedures?'

He nodded as he poured boiling water into two cups that actually had saucers beneath. 'Yes. A lot of eyelifts, nasal augmentation, jaw reshaping—whatever the client wants, really.'

'Do you have a favourite type of surgery?'

He laughed and shook his head. 'The one where my client leaves feeling happy with their results.'

'A politician's answer.' Isla smiled knowingly, taking the cup and saucer from him when he brought it over and sat opposite her.

'A practised answer.' He agreed. 'But one that's true, I'm afraid. People come to me because they're unhappy with what they see on the outside. So if I can make them feel better on the *inside*, then that's what matters to me the most.'

'You have a counsellor on the premises, don't you?'

'We do. Every client that comes to us about needing a cosmetic procedure has to see our surgical counsellor and is given a cooling-down period before they're accepted to surgery. We like to know that they're ready. When you change how you look, when the mirror suddenly shows some-one different, it can have an effect on well-being, even if they thought they wanted the change. Our counsellors are available to our clients for up to a year after their surgery, for no extra charge.'

'That's good.'

'We try to cater to our clients' every need. We adapt to suit them as much as we can.'

Isla smiled and sipped her tea.

'Do you live locally, or…?'

'Near Hammersmith. You?'

'Hampstead Heath.'

'Lovely. Do you have a view of the heath?'

'As a matter of a fact, we do.' He sipped his tea, then glanced at his watch. Some chunky, expensive number sat on his wrist. 'Oops. Better get going. I have a few things to do before surgery. You're happy you know where everything is?'

'If I get lost I can ask someone.'

He stood. Smiled. 'All right. I'll see you in surgery, Isla. I look forward to it.'

'Me too.' She stood as well and watched him go, feeling herself deflate slightly the second he left the room.

At that moment, in walked a male nurse. 'We all feel like that, don't worry.'

'Like what?'

'Like he takes all the air out of the room with him when he goes.'

She blushed. 'Oh, I didn't feel tha—'

'It's fine, honey, honestly. It doesn't help that the guy is single and probably the most eligible millionaire doctor in England right now. Pity he's straight, or I'd try my luck, to be fair. Mind you, wouldn't be the first time I'd turned a straight guy...' The nurse winked, then smiled at her, holding out his hand. 'I'm Justin.'

She laughed. 'Isla. Well, he's not my type, so...'

'Gorgeous, single, rich and clever isn't your type?' Justin took a moment to assess her, looking her up and down. 'Don't tell me...you prefer guys a bit rougher around the edges? Grungy-looking? A bit more blue collar?'

Isla shook her head. She didn't have a type. Not any more. Once upon a time it had been Karl. He'd been tall, dark and clever. A nurse in A & E. They'd bonded over who could tell the grimmest patient story and he'd won. Karl always won. He loved to control things. But he'd not been able to control events. He'd not been able to control that patient's family member that had ruined Isla's life and he'd certainly not been able to control how he felt about it, leading to the breakdown of their marriage. Men had been off her agenda ever since. Isla only ever viewed them as threats now. People to hold at a distance. The best men, in her opinion, were often anaesthetised.

'Let me guess...you're married?'

'Nope. Very much single.'

'Then what's wrong with you, honey?' Justin asked with a laugh as he left the staffroom, chuckling to himself.

Isla grimaced.

Some would say plenty.

Gabe was in the scrub room, getting ready for surgery and gazing through into the theatre at the staff inside.

His patient was already under, the anaesthetist having done their job, hooking the patient up to oxygen and monitoring their stats for any spikes or reactions. The two theatre nurses were busy setting up, Verity showing the new nurse, Isla, how Gabe liked his equipment to be laid out.

He'd met her only briefly, but she seemed to be competent. Phillip wouldn't have hired her if she weren't. She was friendly, he'd been able to talk to her with ease, but there'd been something about her that he couldn't quite put his finger on. It was niggling at him. Worrying away at him, at the base of his skull, as if he wanted to reach inside and scratch at it and make it go away.

What was it?

He liked that she was a natural beauty and did not try to over-emphasise her features. Her hair had been neatly tied back, as regulations expected, but there'd hardly been a lick of make-up on her face. Maybe that was it? He was so used to seeing women so perfectly made-up that when he saw one going au naturel, he noticed?

No, that's not it. It's something else. Why do I feel as if I know her? As if we've met before?

He knew her from somewhere. But if they had met before, then surely she would have mentioned it?

It would come to him. He knew that. Her name was not familiar to him, but it was really annoying to feel this way.

Gabe was a man who prided himself on his memory. He remembered names. Remembered faces. People. Places. So why couldn't he remember someone like her? She said she lived near Hammersmith—well, he'd never been there, but she had worked in a burns unit before and so had he, so maybe they'd worked together once. Maybe she'd been a scrub nurse for him before.

Her gaze met his through the glass and, startled, as if she'd caught him thinking about her, he looked down and away as he finished scrubbing. He needed to get his mind in the game. Needed to be thinking of the rhinoplasty. The patient.

Caron Latimer had come in to get her nose altered. Said that her nose had always bothered her, ever since she was a child. That her siblings had all inherited their mother's petite nose, but she'd inherited her father's Roman nose. She felt that the nasal bridge was too prominent, that her nose was too wide. She wanted something smaller. More like her mother's. She'd brought in pictures of what she wanted.

He'd listened to Caron, advised her. Taken pictures and created a digital model of her nose and then showed her on the computer what her new nose might look like on her face. He'd sent her home with these pictures. Told her to think about it. To talk to their counsellor, to make sure that this was what she wanted.

And she did. She'd lived with a nose that she hated for twenty-three years. It wore down her self-esteem. She felt self-conscious. Her mental health was being affected by it and she'd even taken days off work because some days she just couldn't face going in, because she worked in sales and she often caught customers' gazes focusing on her nose as they talked to her.

So he'd agreed to help her. To reduce the nasal bridge, to reshape her nose so that it was a little smaller and give her a little slope to her nose, rather than an arch.

Caron couldn't wait, she'd said. She'd been so excited when she'd come in this morning at seven a.m. to be prepped for the procedure.

And he couldn't wait to change her life.

That was the part of his job he loved the most. Making a difference. Giving someone a confidence they'd never had before. Making them feel that they could face the world with confidence again. And the work he did here, for the rich and the powerful and, yes, the celebrities, allowed him to fund his trips to India where he worked with acid-attack victims to try and improve their burns. Their scars. To make their lives a little easier.

As he entered Theatre, he looked to Verity, then Isla. 'Are we ready?'

Verity nodded.

The anaesthetist nodded.

Isla nodded.

She had the most beautiful eyes above that scrub mask. If he'd worked with her before, he would have remembered. Isla would have to remain a mystery for a little longer. 'Then let's begin.'

Gabe was a master of his craft and, unlike a lot of surgeons she'd worked with before, who very often ignored everyone around them whilst they were the star of the show, Gabe talked to everyone in the room, explaining what he was doing and why. As if he were in a teaching hospital.

'I'm going to perform a closed rhinoplasty,' he said.

A closed rhinoplasty involved the surgeon making incisions *inside* the nostrils, so that scars would not be shown on the face, rather than an open rhinoplasty in which the surgeon would cut across the skin *between* the nostrils.

'This patient has requested that I make her nose smaller. How do I do that, Verity?'

'By removing or shaving down cartilage and or bone,' she answered, as promptly as a robot.

'This patient also requires some reshaping of her nostrils. How am I going to do that? Isla?' he asked.

She felt a wave of heat wash over her, being put on the spot like this, but she'd seen rhinoplasties performed on accident victims so she felt confident with her answer. 'I assume you will break the nose bone and rearrange the cartilage.' Her cheeks felt hot and she met his gaze above his mask. Happily, she saw the corners of his eyes crease in a smile.

'Correct. And what are some of the risks to the procedure?'

'Breathing problems. Nosebleeds. Infection. Clots. Perhaps even an altered sense of smell.'

She heard Gabe let out a breath, before he nodded. 'Looks like Phillip hired the right person and I didn't need to be there, after all.'

It was a compliment. She had passed the first tests and she was proud of herself. If she could she would have turned to Verity to offer her a high-five, but that wasn't the sort of thing that a professional nurse did in Theatre. Instead Isla stood there knowing that everyone knew she deserved to be there. She might be new, but she was *not* inexperienced and she knew how to handle herself in a theatre.

It took just over two hours for Gabe to be happy he had done enough to reduce the nose to his patient's liking and, once he was done, he asked Isla and Verity to apply the splint and dressings whilst he scrubbed out.

'What did you think?' asked Verity when he'd gone.

'He's an amazing surgeon. Very good!' And she meant it. Watching Gabe work had been a privilege. The way his hands moved, his dexterity, his poise. It had been almost artful.

Verity laughed. 'I meant the surgery, but... okay. You wouldn't be the first nurse to have a crush on Gabriel.'

'I *don't*!' That was two people now who'd implied it was natural to have some secret feelings for Gabe Newton. It was her first day! She didn't need gossip like that carrying around her place of employment. That was not what she was here for! Isla wanted to do her job and nothing more and if that meant proving she was not smitten by Mr Newton's good looks, then she'd damn well show them. 'What surgery is next?' she asked, determined to change the subject.

'Mr Sharma. Buttock augmentation.'

'Right. I'll escort this patient to Recovery. I'll be back soon.'

'Okey doke. See you in a bit.'

'Phillip? What can I do for you?' Gabe had picked up the phone after an internal call had come through on the system.

'Gabe—just checking that you reminded our new theatre nurse about our ritual first-day dinner?'

Gabe closed his eyes in dismay as he realised he'd completely forgotten to mention it. The Garland Clinic had a habit of taking all new employees out for a meal after their first day at the clinic. It was like a welcome. A friendly hello-and-welcome-to-the-team thing. But they'd not had a new member of staff for such a long time, the whole thing had gone completely out of his head. 'Sorry, no. I forgot. Do you want me to go and check with her?'

'Would you, old boy? It's just I'm running a little late. My last patient went a little over time and now I've got a queue and I noticed that your clinic is over.'

'No problem. I'll track her down and ask and then email you.'

'Perfect. Thanks. I've booked a table at Jean Luc's. Seven p.m.'

Gabe brought up the staff rosters on his computer to try and work out where Isla would be. By all accounts she was in theatre with Mohammed, so he made his way there.

When he got there, Mo looked to be about halfway through his procedure. Gabe pressed the button on the intercom. 'Hi, I just wondered if I might have a quick word with our fabulous new nurse.'

Mo looked up over the patient to Isla and nodded.

Verity took her place as Isla walked over to the viewing window. She looked confused. A little worried.

'Something wrong?'

'No, nothing's wrong.' He smiled, to show he wasn't a threat, or a problem of any kind. 'Are you okay for dinner this evening?'

She blinked. 'Dinner? Oh, um…'

He watched as she went from shocked to desperate. Desperate to turn him down, and that was when he realised that maybe he'd phrased the question wrong. 'The new employee's dinner. With *everyone* there. Not just me,' he added quietly, almost feeling a blush come upon himself.

Isla stared at him as realisation hit. 'Oh! That! I remember Mr Garland mentioning it at interview, I'd forgotten. Um…well, yes. Yes! I can make the dinner. What time is it?'

'Reservation is at seven o'clock. Jean Luc's.'

'Right. Right. Dress code?'

'Smart.'

She continued to nod.

'So, that's a yes? I can tell Phil that you'll be there?'

'Yes!' She laughed. 'I thought for a minute there that you, that you were...' She laughed again, looked away. 'Seven is fine, though it might be a bit of a stretch for me to get home in time to change.'

'I'm sure we can let you go home a little early just this once.'

As she headed back to the surgery, Gabe came away from Theatre feeling slightly strange. Perturbed. What had just happened? She'd thought that *he* was asking *her* out personally!

He almost laughed, until he remembered that she'd been working out how she could possibly turn him down and that stopped him in his tracks. He wasn't used to women turning him down. Normally, they all said yes. Or asked him themselves.

But Isla had been going to say no. Politely. Nicely. Without hurting his feelings.

And that just made him like her all the more.

CHAPTER TWO

SHE'D BEEN ALLOWED to leave early, so that she could get home in time to change and get to the dinner. She'd looked up Jean Luc's on the Internet and stared open-mouthed at the prices for a while, before thanking her lucky stars that Mr Garland had told her when she'd accepted the posting that the clinic paid for the new employee's dinner.

I mean, thank God. If I had to pay, we'd be at the local pizza place.

Not that there was anything wrong with Mario's Pizza. She'd had many a happy night in front of the television, chowing down on a pepperoni taste sensation. There was no pizza on the menu at Jean Luc's. There wasn't much on the menu at Jean Luc's that she understood at all. Most of it was in French and she'd never remembered much of her French from school except for *je m'appelle* and she wasn't sure how far that would get her tonight.

Mr Garland and the other consultants, Mr Sharma and Mr Newton, were no doubt built for this sort of dining. A la carte. It wasn't really her thing and when she'd first heard about it, she'd actually tried to get out of it.

'Splendid! We're so glad you've accepted the job. Just a little heads up, the partners always take a new member of staff out for dinner after their first day. Special treat. A sort of welcome aboard the good ship Garland!'

She'd panicked. The idea of having to go to dinner with three men that she didn't know had terrified her.

'Oh, I'm not sure that I—'

'Don't worry!' he'd interrupted. *'You won't just have us there, the admin and other nursing staff will be there, too.'*

To be fair, that had made it a little easier. If the other staff were there, she'd feel a little more relaxed. Less like a mouse surrounded by three big cats.

The question was, what was she to wear? She'd only ever had a nurse's salary and, recently, she'd only been working part-time, so she'd not had much money to spare on cocktail dresses. She had two options to choose from. A little black dress that had saved her bacon on a number of occasions and a sleeveless, strapless white dress that clung to her figure and that she'd bought before her life had changed for evermore and she wasn't sure if she would ever wear it.

The white dress made a statement. The white dress ought to be worn by a woman who was comfortable in her own skin. The white dress was confidence.

She'd bought it years ago, when she had felt like a badass. When she had felt indestructible and that nothing on this earth could hurt her.

But then it had.

Isla stared at them both. She could hide in the black dress. Pair it with a short black cardigan and kitten heels and if she added some jewellery, a necklace, some dangly earrings, maybe she'd get away with it looking more expensive than it actually was.

But her gaze kept getting pulled back to the white dress.

Jean Luc's demanded this dress. The Garland consultants demanded this dress. An all-expenses-paid à-la-carte dinner demanded this dress. This dress might make her feel…what? Better? More confident? Or would she feel as if she had a target on her back? Because *guys* would look at her in this dress.

She decided to put it on. Just to see what it would look like in the safety of her own home. Just to see if it would fit still.

I mean, it's been a few years. I've probably put on some pounds…

But it did fit.

It fitted like a glove. It made her shoulders and her arms look great. Yes, she'd been working out lately, figuring that physical strength was important if she was to start going back out into the world. The skirt ended just above her knees and had a small split on the left-hand side. Slipping her feet into a pair of nude heels made her legs look as if they went on for days. Even her calves were shapely!

She'd not noticed before. Normally when she studied herself in front of a mirror she was at the gym, in shorts and a tee shirt and sweating profusely and checking her form as she lifted weights. She'd never turned this way. Or that. Or pointed her toes in heels.

It's too much. I look way too much!

She almost took it off, so that she could retreat to the safety of the black dress, but a shawl in her wardrobe took that moment to slither off its hanger and make itself known and she knelt to pick it up and wrapped it around her shoulders, allowing herself to hide somewhat behind its silver fringing, and she just knew, in that moment, that she didn't ever want to go back to that little black dress.

The white dress stuck two fingers up at all that she had gone through before and this was her new life. Her new start. So why not start it with confidence?

Isla picked up her mobile and dialled for a taxi before she lost her nerve.

Phillip had reserved for them the large oval table near the bay window and, as usual, was revelling in his role as host as Gabe joined them, Mohammed, Jane, Justin and Verity, greeting them all, dropping kisses onto the cheeks of the women and shaking hands and patting the backs of the men.

'Our guest of honour hasn't arrived yet,' said Phil as he saw him look around the table to the empty chair beside him.

'Oh. Maybe I should wait for her at the door?'

'No, no, the maître d' knows that we're waiting for her. He'll bring her straight to the table when she arrives. I take it her first day went well?'

Gabe nodded, settling into his seat. 'Very well, yes. I certainly had no problems—she was an excellent help in Theatre. Very knowledgeable. Professional.'

'Good! Good.' Phil sipped at his glass of water.

A waiter came to take their drinks order, but they asked him to wait until Isla arrived and as the waiter disappeared into the kitchen, Gabe's gaze fell upon movement by the entrance, where a woman had come in wearing a white dress.

He could view her only from behind, but she had beautiful honey-blonde hair that fell in a wave to just past her shoulders. She wore a wrap, or maybe it was a shawl, in silver that glittered and caught the light of all the candles in the room as she leant in to speak to the maître d'.

And then she turned to follow him in and Gabe realised, with shock, that it was Isla, their new theatre nurse.

'Wow.'

Heads turned at the table to see whom he was looking at and somehow he'd got to his feet without realising it. Phillip and Mohammed stood too and suddenly Isla was there, smiling, blushing, greeting the partners and all the staff and then she was in front of him, looking shy and tentative, and he leaned in to kiss her hello on the cheek and it was as if everything were in slow motion.

Her smile. Her eyes. Smoky and seductive.

Her scent. Light. Floral.

She looked...breathtaking! Completely unlike the woman he'd met today in the hall reception at the Garland Clinic. This Isla wore make-up and though she'd been beautiful without it, with the make-up, he was astounded. Drawn in to those soft blue eyes of hers, the way she looked at him from under those thick, dark lashes. Pulled to her soft pink lips, full and inviting, slicked with gloss. Magnetised by her womanly figure. A perfect hourglass.

Shocked, he looked away from her to see if she was having the same effect on everyone else, but instead he just found Justin looking at him with one eyebrow raised and an amused smile upon his mouth. That guy missed nothing.

And then they were seated and ordering drinks and the waiter disappeared again, this time to fulfil their order.

'You look wonderful,' he said, feeling the need to compliment her. 'Not that you didn't earlier on, but tonight is just…wonderful.' He laughed, embarrassed at his own inability to come up with another adjective.

'Thank you. You look *wonderful*, too.'

He'd thrown on his usual tuxedo. He'd had it made especially by Hugo Knight, a bespoke tailor in London who dressed a lot of male stars and celebrities.

'You, er…found this place, all right?'

She smiled. 'Not my job. I left that to the taxi driver, I'm afraid.'

'Of course.' *Idiot.*

'I'd like to propose a toast,' said Phillip, raising his glass, after the waiter had returned with their drinks. 'To Isla, our new theatre nurse! We are so very happy to have you join us and we hope that you will have many happy years with us at the Garland. We promise to try not to be too demanding. To Isla!'

'To Isla!' Gabe concurred, clinking his flute with everyone else's even though he'd read somewhere that clinking glasses was actually bad etiquette. You were only meant to raise your glass. But as Phillip and all the others were doing so, he knew he would feel bad if he didn't join them in the practice.

'Thank you, everyone. For making me feel so welcome.' Isla sipped her champagne as the waiter arrived with menus.

Gabe was looking at his for a moment when he realised that Isla looked a little confused.

'So it's true, then?' he asked, with a smile.

'What's that?'

'That even though your surname is French, it doesn't actually mean that you can read French?'

She blushed. 'I can read it. I just can't understand a word it says. Can you help me?' she whispered. 'I don't want to seem ignorant.'

He smiled back, amused. 'Of course. Let's see, there are three starters to choose from. There are mussels. Or there's a tomato and basil tarte tatin, or you can choose soupy cheese.'

Isla laughed. 'You make it sound so delicious!'

'I didn't say I was a perfect translator, but I understand the general gist.'

'Hmm, what are you going to have?'

'The soupy cheese. It's Gruyère and Camembert. I've had it from here before and it's fabulous.'

She nodded. 'Then I'll do the same. Mains?'

'Okay, let's see…five options: posh chicken casserole…posh steak and chips…posh fish quiche…posh fish on its own or a fig and ham salad.'

He could see that she was enjoying his tongue-in-cheek translation.

'Posh chicken casserole, I think.'

'Perfect choice. I'll join you.'

The waiter took everyone's order and disappeared back into the kitchen. Gabe couldn't help but smile as he was really beginning to enjoy himself, which was a surprise. He never usually enjoyed these employee dinners. He often found them to be very formal, very polite, the new employee not sure how to behave or what to talk about, and he often discovered that the dinner turned almost into a secondary interview with the new employee sharing their life story to date. He hoped that Isla wouldn't get interrogated that way, especially by Justin, who could be a bit persistent in his search for gossip.

'So…tell us *all* about yourself, Isla,' said Justin, right on cue. 'The bosses here know a little about you, but I'm totally in the dark. I've already asked around, but everyone's so light on the details!'

'What do you want to know?' asked Isla, smiling.

'Well, who you are. Where you came from. That kind of thing.'

'All right, well, um, I've always been a nurse. It was all I ever wanted to be from school. I don't know why. No one else in my family had worked in medicine. My first posting was in A & E, which I liked. Nice. Fast-paced. Huge variety of patients, which I liked. Occasionally, I got to work in Theatre and realised that I loved that the most, so I did some extra training and here I am.'

Justin nodded, lips pursed as if he was considering the information carefully. 'And you're here alone tonight. Should we infer from that that you're single?' He waggled his eyebrows.

'Yes and happily so.'

'Pretty thing like you? Won't take long, I'm sure.'

Gabe couldn't help but notice the impertinent wink Justin gave him when Isla took a sip of her drink. He knew the implication, but he would never choose to date a colleague and he was in no position to date anyone. Not with his situation. Not with Bea. It was all too complicated and that was why he *only* went on *first dates* with women. If they could even be called dates, that was. He gave women who wanted to be seen with him a good time. A great meal, fabulous conversation, maybe a bit of dancing, but then he waved them goodbye. The women he got spotted out and about around town with were not the kind of women who would be able to deal with Bea, his daughter.

They came as a package and they were a complicated package. Dating, falling in love, were not on his agenda, thank you very much. The women he was seen with used him, as much as he used them. For mutual exposure.

'I'm not really looking for anyone right now,' Isla said.

Phew. Good. That let him off the hook.

'Why ever not?' Justin pushed. He really was on form tonight.

She shrugged and Gabe could tell she was feeling as if she had her back against the wall. Justin really could be a horrific snoop, so he decided to rescue her.

'I think it's a good thing. To be single. You can live your life your own way. By your own rules.'

Isla looked gratefully towards him and nodded. 'Absolutely.'

'Well, you would say that, Gabe. Don't think I haven't seen what you get up to most weeks. I see your face every month in that celebrity gossip rag. I think Mack Desveaux is obsessed with you.'

Mack Desveaux. The bane of his life. A kid he went to school with, who'd always been on the periphery of his life until he'd discovered that when he'd begun to date Ellis, she'd also been seeing someone else—Mack. When she'd realised her feelings for Gabe, she'd ended it with Mack, but Mack had never ended it with Gabe. Hounding him relentlessly as if he just couldn't get past his losing to him. 'I can't control the free press, Justin. *You* should know that,' he said, taking a sip of his own drink.

Justin blushed. He'd once been dragged into the press because he'd attended a charity ball that had also been attended by some minor pop-star celebrities and he'd off-handedly been rude to one, snatched her mobile phone from her hand and thrown it into a swimming pool because he'd thought the young woman had been flirting with the guy that he liked.

'Yes, well…'

Isla turned to Gabe, one eyebrow raised, intrigued, and he figured he'd just tell her later. But he wouldn't let Justin bully her. The guy could be awful sometimes if he was bored.

At that moment, the food arrived and their Gruyère and Camembert fondue was placed before them. It smelt divine and came with two little side pots filled with croutons and perfectly cubed types of bread. Sourdough. Rye. Plain white. Wholemeal. One with sun-dried tomatoes in and what tasted like cranberries.

It was delicious!

'Nice?' he asked Isla.

'It's gorgeous! Thank you for the recommendation.'

'No problem.' He didn't know why he'd felt

the need to take her under his wing and protect her from the vultures. Gabe just knew that it felt good. This wasn't the type of place Isla was used to. He could tell. She didn't seem comfortable at all and she'd come here alone, all quietly spoken and shy, yet still rocking that amazing white dress.

He couldn't help but notice how good she looked in it. He'd not noticed her figure at work, but, then again, she'd been in scrubs mostly, a hairnet, a face mask. Tonight, she wore the dress, the dress did not wear her, and she looked stunning. Clearly she took care of her body. Arms and legs didn't get that toned just from working in Theatre. You had to work at it. He knew, having spent hours in a gym himself. Though a lot of his gym use was because he felt angry, or that there'd been an injustice with his life, or whenever Bea had a relapse and he felt frustrated. He'd lift weights or pound the treadmill until sweat dripped off him and he would only stop when he felt exhausted. It probably wasn't good to work out that way, but it had been working for him so far.

'Maybe now that he's got some food in front of him, he'll stop interrogating you,' he said in a quiet aside.

Isla flushed. 'It's fine.'

'No. It's not.' He met her gaze. Conspiratorially.

Sideways. Quick. A glimpse. But it was enough to cause a strange sensation inside him. As if he'd been hit. By a wave of something. Warmth. Affection.

No. Something stronger than affection.

Gabe frowned and speared a piece of bread and dipped it in cheese as he tried to analyse what was happening. He didn't like it. Didn't welcome it. He'd not felt this since he'd met his wife. Before she was his wife.

No. No. That's not it. It can't be the same.

Gabe dabbed at his lips with a napkin and took another fortifying drink of the champagne. His glass was nearly empty and now he felt like the one trapped in a corner.

Was Justin staring at him? Was Isla? Anyone else?

Isla thankfully now took control of the conversation and directed a question to Phillip, asking him about how he started the Garland Clinic.

As his senior partner and friend began pontificating about his great start in life, Gabe found himself retreating and glancing at his mobile phone, in case there were any urgent messages he needed to respond to. He wouldn't be the first consultant to walk out on the new-employee dinner because of some crisis at home.

But there wasn't a crisis, because no one was at home. Bea was at boarding school, as she always was Monday to Fridays, coming home only at the weekends. Suddenly he missed her. Missed his daughter like crazy and wished they were at home together, so he could sit in her bedroom and read her a story, the way he'd used to when she was little. Before she'd decided that she hated him.

When was the last time he read to her? He couldn't think. Couldn't remember. This feeling that he felt for Isla was confusing matters. Playing with his brain. 'Excuse me,' he said, getting up from the table and heading out to the veranda to get some fresh air and some perspective. Maybe it was the dress? Her eyes? Her scent? Her vulnerability?

Something…

Maybe it was all of those things and more.

Or maybe it's because I've not let anyone get close for far too long and, by my protecting her from Justin, she sneaked past my barricades?

Gabe leant against the stone and looked down into the gardens that were filled with flowers and blooms and fat bumble bees that were getting their last evening collection of pollen.

'Are you okay?'

He spun around at her voice, surprised. He'd not expected her to follow him out here.

Justin will have noticed. Damn it.

'Yeah. Yeah! I'm good. Just…needed a bit of

fresh air, is all. It can get a little stuffy in there, sometimes…' He hoped he sounded convincing.

'Me too. I wasn't following you, though, so please don't think that. I wasn't even sure if you'd come out here. I just asked the waiter if there was somewhere *I* could go.'

He nodded, understanding. 'How are you enjoying your employee dinner?'

'Nerve-racking. I almost didn't come at all. This isn't my thing.'

'No. Nor me.' He sighed.

Isla frowned. 'Really? I always see you out and about.' Then she flushed. 'In the magazines. I know, I'm sorry. I shouldn't pay any attention to those, but my mother brings them round and… I know I shouldn't believe everything I see or read.'

'No, it's fine. Honestly, I get that a lot. A lot of my clients tell me the same thing. I'm kinda used to it.'

'Did you really go out for dinner once with Elizabeth Traynor?' she asked him, curiously.

Gabe laughed. 'Yes. But! It wasn't like it was shown. Celeb photographs and cosmetic surgery are very much the same. It's all about perception and what you can't see.'

She took a step towards him, looked over the veranda, then back at him. 'What didn't I see?'

'That we were at a party thrown by her agent. A woman called Cecelia Trent, who'd wanted us to meet to talk about Elizabeth getting some subtle nose work. And that there were a hundred or so *other* people there. That snapshot made it look like we were having some secret romantic rendezvous, but in reality we had loads of other people around us. They'd been cut out of shot.' Which was what Mack had intended. He'd seemed to make it his life's mission to paint Gabe as some sort of Lothario, when it blatantly wasn't true. To paint him as someone women shouldn't trust. But rich, handsome playboy doctor sold copies much better than doctor attends party.

Isla laughed. 'I see. Sorry.'

'It's okay. Just don't believe everything you see.'

'From now on, I will question everything. Maybe if I'd done that earlier, then my life wouldn't have gone to pot.'

He frowned. 'How so?'

Isla shook her head rapidly. 'It's nothing. Forget it. We all make mistakes, right?'

'We do. We're human. I think it's expected of us. Otherwise we'd be perfect and no one wants perfection, do they?'

She laughed, grateful to him for letting her off the hook. 'No. Though maybe don't tell your clients that.'

'No.' He watched as she leaned against the veranda. The way the white dress hugged her body, a small split in a side seam revealing a hint of thigh that made him feel all hot for some reason.

I cannot have some sort of crush on the new theatre nurse!

He had to end this. Stop it in its tracks. 'We should go back inside. Justin'll be wondering where we both are, or putting two and two together and coming up with five.'

'Right. Well, you go first. If we go back together that would definitely stir a pot.'

'Absolutely.' He pushed himself off the veranda and, without thinking, without realising what he was doing, he touched her fingers with his, in some sort of acknowledgement, as he passed her. A quick touch. A brief entwining of fingers.

Wait. What did I just do that for?

A gesture of support? Hopefully she saw it that way.

He entered the restaurant, feeling his face flaming with heat, and he stopped, out of sight of the veranda, out of sight of the table, and just took a moment to loosen his tie, to check his cuffs, to regain control over himself, before he put himself back out on display. Forcing a smile, he headed back to the table.

'Everything all right?' asked Phillip.

'Yes. Fine. Mmm-hmm,' he said, settling into his seat. 'Where's Isla?' he asked, to try and imply that they'd not just spent some time together alone on the veranda.

'Got a bit hot, or something,' Phillip replied. 'We figured you'd finished your starter, so we let the waiter take it away. Hope that was all right?'

'Yes, fine.' He'd forgotten about the food. Forgotten whereabouts they were in dinner. Two more courses to go. Two more courses and then he could plead work the next day and go home. Get some much-needed space from the new theatre nurse and some much-needed control over his responses.

'Actually, might I ask you a favour, Gabe?'

'Sure, what's up?'

'Well, I've had a long day and fancy a bit of an early night tonight—please the wife, you know how it is—and Mo needs to get back to his babysitter. I think Justin and the others want to go on to a godawful club or something, but Isla said she wants an early night… Would it be an awful imposition if I asked you to wait with her until her taxi arrived to take her home later on?'

'That's fine,' he said. Even though it wasn't fine.

It wasn't fine at all.

What would he say to her, standing out there, on the street, with her alone? He couldn't leave her there. It was the gentlemanly thing to do.

I just won't stand so close. Won't look her in the eye. Maybe I should apologise for the hand thing?

At that moment, Isla came back to the table and all the men, Gabe, Phillip, Mohammed, Justin, got up to stand, until she was seated.

'Everything all right, Isla?' Justin asked.

'Good, thank you.'

'Excellent.'

He sounded smug. Justin sounded as though he could see every little thought in Gabe's head and somehow knew about them meeting on the veranda.

Gabe couldn't look at him right now.

So he downed the rest of his champagne and poured himself some more.

CHAPTER THREE

THE LATE EVENING breeze was beginning to feel a little chilly. Isla was glad of her shawl as she pulled it close around her shoulders.

'Cold?'

'A little.'

'Here.' Gabe began to remove his dinner jacket.

'Oh, you don't need to do that!' she began to protest, even though she was grateful for the gesture and the warmth of his jacket instantly made her feel better. 'Thanks. It was nice of you to wait with me, but I'll be okay. You can go, if you'd like.' She was nervous. The two of them standing there, outside the restaurant. It had been a long time since she'd been outside with a man, alone, at night and the situation made her nervous. Even more nervous since that moment on the veranda when his fingers had caressed hers as he'd passed her by.

A jolt of electricity had shot up her arm, awareness spreading through her, making her feel something she'd not felt for a very long time.

Want. Need.

It was disturbing. Terrifying, almost. And with her boss! If there was one place you did not want to conduct a romance, it was at your job, because when it didn't work out, it could make life extremely difficult. And Isla felt as if she carried enough baggage already, without the bumpy road that a crush on her boss would entail. There was an imbalance of power in that relationship and that was fine when it was just work, because some people were meant to be in charge, but there shouldn't be an imbalance in an intimate relationship.

But his jacket felt so good around her shoulders and she appreciated the gentlemanly gesture. And she could inhale his scent. Damn, the man not only looked good, but smelled delicious, too! It was not helping with the inappropriate feelings! And he stood there, looking gorgeous in his white shirt and undone bow tie, hands in his pockets, as if he were about to walk a runway.

'This must seem a boring night for you,' she said.

Gabe turned to look at her, confused. He had been looking up and down the street as they waited for her taxi they'd ordered twenty minutes earlier, because he'd thought he'd seen something. 'Boring? Why?'

'Out with colleagues. Having to babysit me, when you could be out and about with some actors or models. Sipping champagne in penthouse suites and partying till the early hours.'

He smiled. 'Is that what you think happens?'

'Isn't it?'

He laughed. 'Well, yeah, but don't ever make the mistake of thinking that they're not boring. Those sorts of places are all the same. The *people* are all the same. They're networking, selling themselves and some of them are letting off steam in the worst ways possible.'

'If you don't enjoy it, why do you go to those places?'

'I get invited and it would be rude to say no, and sometimes I go because I haven't been out all week, or I had a difficult weekend and need to blow off steam myself.'

'Why would you have a difficult weekend?'

He shrugged. 'I don't. Not really. Perhaps difficult is the wrong word to use. I, er…have a young daughter. Beatrice. We, er—how shall I say this?—have a difference in communication style.'

'Oh. A pre-teen. Must be challenging sometimes? Is she at home?'

'No. She attends boarding school in the week. She comes home on Fridays, goes back Sunday evenings.' He looked up the road again as a car's lights illuminated the street as it turned the corner. 'This looks like you.'

He said he sometimes had difficult weekends. His daughter was at home weekends. Did they not get along? Some dads found it difficult to be with their daughters. Found they were having problems bonding, perhaps? She knew because that was what she'd experienced with her own father. He'd been in the army and had often been posted away for long periods of time and when he had come home, it was as if he hadn't known how to be a civilian. Hadn't known how to talk to her and so he hadn't bothered. She'd yearned so much for her dad to give her a hug, to tell her he loved her, that he was proud of her, to take an interest in her life, but he never had. Or had never been able to breach that chasm between them. He'd died never truly having had a proper, in-depth conversation with her about anything of note.

The taxi was pulling up in front of them. Isla shrugged off Gabe's jacket, to give it back to him. She stepped close, smiling, handing it back, her mouth forming a thank you, when suddenly there was a shout from behind them.

'Gabriel!'

They both turned and Gabe swore softly. 'Damn! Hide!'

Hide? There was nothing she could do but raise his jacket to shadow her face as the whole street suddenly lit up with a flash of a photo being taken. Isla suddenly felt frightened, frozen to the spot, Gabe's jacket over the top of her head as Gabe himself swung open the taxi door and told her to get in quick.

Isla did so, clambering in, but she didn't want to leave him out there, all alone, without his jacket, with the paparazzi, and she called to him. 'Get in the car!'

Gabe looked at her, startled, then got in with her and he yelled at the taxi driver to just get going.

The car engine roared and they escaped, Gabe settling back into the seat with a sigh and an order for the taxi driver to go to Hammersmith. Then he turned to her. 'Sorry about that. Someone from the restaurant must have called someone, or texted someone, and then that happened.'

'How do you even live like that? Knowing someone could take your picture at any moment?'

She passed him his jacket back and he shrugged it on. 'I've got used to it. I don't like it, so I don't go out much. It got worse after I was snapped with Elizabeth Traynor. They thought they had a great fairy tale they could peddle. England's finest actress, single, beautiful, seen with eligible widower, out on the town.' He shook his head. 'It's what they chase. The fairy tale. Imagined relationships. Romances. It sells copies and ruins lives. But they don't care about that last part.'

'I'm sorry they do that to you. Do you think

they got a good picture?' She hated the idea that she might now appear in some gossip mag: *Gabriel Newton's Mystery Woman!*

'I hope not, but I guess we'll find out.'

'Whereabouts in Hammersmith, love?' asked the taxi driver.

'Penny Road. Next to the Black Bridge pub.'

Gabe leant forward and passed a large note to the driver. 'Appreciate you keeping this quiet, all right?'

'Will do, mate.' The driver took the note and slipped it into his shirt pocket.

It was all very cloak and dagger. Isla wasn't sure how to feel and so she did what she always did. She giggled. Then laughed. Holding her belly, because it hurt so much as she guffawed at the whole situation, Gabe joining her. For a moment there, she'd thought she was in danger, but she hadn't been, and Gabe had rescued her and thrown her into a taxi and now he was paying that taxi driver to keep his silence! It was incredible! 'I never thought the evening would turn out like this,' she said, once she'd got her breath back. Breathing, trying to regain her composure.

Gabe was smiling. 'Nor me. Strangely. I'm sorry you got dragged into my mess.'

'It's okay. I had fun tonight, which was something I'd not expected.' And it was true. She'd not expected to enjoy a single moment of it. When had she last enjoyed herself like that? When had she last belly-laughed like that? Not for *years*. She looked at Gabe, because she wanted him to see that she wasn't offended. She wasn't upset.

He looked back at her. Those dark blue eyes of his twinkling in the shadows of the car. His hesitant half-smile. His gaze dropping to her mouth and then back to her eyes.

Isla swallowed as the mood shifted in the car. Felt herself grow hot.

'I've never been rescued by a maiden before,' he said softly.

She coloured, feeling heat bloom in her cheeks. Her neck. Her chest. Feeling butterflies swirl in her stomach. 'It was my pleasure. To be honest with you, I've always felt like the one that needed rescuing.'

He was staring so intently at her that they didn't notice the car pull to a stop.

She was so busy staring into his eyes, allowing herself to drown in them, that she didn't even hear the taxi driver clear his throat and say, 'We're here, love.'

Gabe's hand reached up. Tentative. Slow. He caressed her cheek, his hand against her skin sending bolts of lightning through her body as she came alive, her breath catching in her throat.

'Ten quid. When you're ready.'

The driver's voice cut through the moment this

time and Isla suddenly started and turned away, embarrassed, blushing. She pushed open the car door and reached into her clutch bag to pay the driver.

'I've got it. Don't worry,' said Gabe.

'No, I must pay. I—'

'It's fine. Honestly. Go inside.' Gabe had clambered from the car, too and stood behind her as she fumbled in her bag, this time for the keys to her friend's flat where she was currently staying until she could find a place of her own. She could feel the gazes of both men and it made her clumsy, the keys dropping to the floor.

Gabe reached them before she could and then, when they were both standing again, he passed them over.

She smiled at him, thankful, and inserted the key into her lock and opened the door.

Was she to ask him in for coffee?

No. She couldn't possibly do that.

'Thank you. For a…lovely evening,' she managed.

'Good night, Isla. I'll see you tomorrow,' he said, clearly waiting to make sure she got inside safely.

She gave him a nod and stepped inside, closing the door shut behind her and flicking the switch up on the lock to double-secure it. Isla let out a long breath and let her clutch drop to the floor.

She kicked off her heels, then made her way up the stairs, feeling incredibly drained and unsure of what had just happened.

She and Gabe had had a moment.

A true, heart-stopping moment! And not just once, either! That moment at the restaurant, when he'd brushed past her on the veranda and his fingers had caressed hers. The way he'd protected her with the journalist and then the moment in the car.

He was going to kiss me!

What did that mean for them now? How were they going to work together?

Maybe I should go into his consulting room tomorrow? Ask for a private word? Tell him that nothing will come of it and that we'd both just been caught up in a moment?

Isla refused to get caught up in any fairy tale.

Because something bad always happened to the princess.

CHAPTER FOUR

'I THINK I just look tired. A bit droopy. I need you to give my eyes back their youthful appearance, because I used to be offered roles on television that were for daughters or young wives and the last role I got offered? Menopausal mother! I swear the next one that comes in will be for someone's granny.'

Gabriel smiled sympathetically. 'Have you had any eye surgery before?' he asked as he came around his desk to examine the face of a minor television celebrity who'd once had the recurring role in a soap opera of a wayward twenty-something.

'Not my eyes. Botox in my forehead. Lip fillers. Nothing more than that.'

He nodded. To him? Her eyes looked fine. Perfect for her age. Cleo Jones was in her late thirties, according to the press. In her medical file? Forty-three. But she did have ptosis, a little excess skin on her upper eyelid. The bags under her eyes, hidden by make-up, made her eyes look a little asymmetrical, so he could correct that. 'Have you ever been diagnosed with dry eyes? Or any type of eye condition?'

'No. I wear glasses to read.'

'That's fine. And do you smoke?'

'Socially.'

'It would be best if you could stop before the surgery as smoking can really have an effect on the speed of the recovery process.'

'Consider it done,' she replied. 'Anything to get better roles.'

Gabe sat back down and went through Cleo's medical history, past issues, if she was on any current medications. He performed a detailed examination of her eyes, her eyelids, her facial skin and assessed the underlying tissues. He took photographs from all angles and fed the images into the computer to show her what her eyes might look like post-surgery.

'That looks great!' she said.

'You understand that these are the optimum outcomes for surgery, but every surgery carries a risk. Blepharoplasty is a safe operation, relatively, and offers many aesthetic benefits, but it still carries a risk of infection, swelling, eye problems, bruising or even secondary surgery.'

'I do. I know you have to tell me the risks. But look at what happens to me and my career if I don't have this surgery. I lose work. I lose the best roles and you have no idea what that will do to my current state of mental health. I can't keep losing out to Petra.' He had no idea who Petra was, but assumed it was another actress.

'Well, let's schedule another appointment in two weeks. This will give you time to think about the procedure, read up on the risks and have some time to speak to our on-site counsellor.'

'I don't need a shrink.'

'Maybe not, but they are there to discuss any concerns you may have.'

'Two weeks? And then I'll have the surgery?'

'If you're still keen to go ahead, we'll get you booked in.'

'Good.' Cleo stood and reached across the table to shake his hand. 'I was told you're the best.'

'And the awards show last year told me that you were the best supporting actress.'

Cleo groaned. 'Supporting actress! I gave that role my all. I should have got lead actress.'

'Well, maybe this year? Or the next? Once you've recovered.'

She smiled. 'I shall hold you to that, Gabriel. We should meet for drinks one time. I'm having a birthday party in August. You should come.'

'Thank you.'

'I'll get Martin to send you an invite. Save the date!'

'I certainly will.' He said goodbye to Cleo and

had gone to write up his notes when there was a knock at his door. 'Come in!' He didn't look up to see who it was. He figured it was probably Jane with a tray. She normally came at this time with tea or coffee and some biscuits.

'Can I have a word?'

Not Jane.

He glanced up. Swallowed hard.

It was Isla. Looking all nervous and anxious. Unable to meet his gaze. She looked...traumatised. It was the only word for it.

'Sure. Take a seat.' He indicated the recently vacated chair left by Cleo.

'No, thanks. I'll stand. This won't take a minute.'

Isla had lain awake all night, thinking. Listening to police sirens go past, patrons from the pub stumbling out of the door and making their way down the street. All the time, just staring up at the shadows on the ceiling, but not really seeing it. Instead, her brain had given her snatches of images. Thoughts. Feelings. The way Gabe had looked when she'd entered the restaurant. The way he'd leaned in to kiss her cheek. Phillip and Mohammed had done the same thing, too, but her brain wasn't rerunning *those* moments. The way Gabe had looked at her on the veranda right before he'd left, the brush of his fingers against hers, the way he'd leaned in towards her at the table in the restaurant to help her translate the French menu.

The way he'd looked at her in the taxi. Stroked her cheek. Gazed at her mouth.

That was day one. Day one of employment and already it was getting complicated and she *did not need* complicated in her life. She'd had that. Been paralysed by that. Had pressed pause on her life to deal with everything. She did not need Gabe to be another complication.

And so she'd got up that morning, determined to start this day afresh. She would eat, get dressed, go into work and be the best surgical nurse the Garland Clinic had ever seen! The thought had propelled her, rejuvenated her, had even made her feel that everything would be all right.

Until she'd opened her front door.

'I won't take up too much of your time,' she said, feeling a million emotions broiling away.

'It's fine.'

She nodded. Managed a smile that disappeared as fast as it came. All night she'd been rehearsing what she'd say. All morning, whilst she'd struggled to force down some breakfast.

Until she'd opened her front door.

But now that she was here, now that she was standing before him, it was as though all of those words, all of those fine sentences she'd constructed, had got clogged up in her throat at once. 'I'm just a theatre nurse. I'm just here to do my job and for you to be my boss.' She paused, needing to swallow down her nerves. 'Last night... last night a few things happened and those roles, those boundaries somehow...' She couldn't think of how to end that sentence.

'They got blurred,' he said, rescuing her.

Isla nodded. 'Yes. Yes, they did, and I don't think I can cope with...blurred.' She frowned, not sure if that sentence made any sense, but feeling it *somehow* did. 'Blurred is not for me. I need my life to be simple. Plain. Boring. To go to work, to do a good job and then to go home again. I don't need any more than that. I don't need to open my front door and have a bunch of journalists waiting to fire questions at me and take my picture!'

He stared back at her. Appalled. 'They found you.'

'Yes, they bloody well did! And they were waiting for me to come out! Waiting for me, like vultures, desperate to snatch at some scrap of meat left on the bones. Who was I? What was I to you? Whether we were serious!'

'I guess the taxi driver didn't keep his mouth shut, after all.'

She looked at him, blinking, surprised. She'd expected something more. She'd expected protests. She'd expected...what? Not this. Not this acceptance of everything she'd said. 'The taxi driver? That's what you're worried about? I had to run back inside my flat and hide. I had to clamber down the fire escape at the back, with an overnight bag, because I'm afraid they'll be waiting for me when I go back home! I've spent the morning calling friends I haven't spoken to in ages, looking for another place to stay, but no one's got anywhere and now I don't know what to do!'

He paused for a moment. Looked a little awkward, as if to imply that his next sentence would only cause her more problems. 'I take it you've not seen what's online either, then?'

She blinked some more. Online? What did that have to do with...? *Oh, God! The paparazzi!* 'No.'

Isla watched, mute, as Gabe tapped at the screen and brought up the site of celebrity journalist, Mack Desveaux, and showed it to her. She stared and felt all of the air in her lungs leave her body as if in one breath. There she was, in picture form, behind Gabe, her face obscured by her shawl as she clambered into the taxi, Gabe obstructing most of the picture with his palm out to block the camera. The headline was *Who is Gabe's Mystery Woman?*

'Oh, my God...' She leaned against his desk and began to read the story beneath it.

Last night Gabriel Newton, thirty-eight, eligible bachelor, widower and millionaire, was seen

outside exclusive restaurant Jean Luc's with a
mystery blonde woman, who managed to escape
into a taxi before her identity could be captured.

Questions mount as to who she might be.
Gabriel is often photographed with some
of the country's most beautiful women and
he has never, to our knowledge, protected
the identity of his female partners, so what
makes this one so special? Ideas speculate
whether London's most famously single cos-
metic surgeon has finally found someone to
settle down with, since the terrible passing
of his beautiful wife, Ellis, with whom he had
a daughter, now twelve.

If you can help us identify this woman,
then please get in touch.

Isla read the article twice, three times, before
she lifted her gaze and stared at Gabe. 'I don't
believe this!'

'You're in shock, I know. I can only apologise
that you have been dragged into this.' He sighed.
'Let me get you some tea. Tea is good for shock.'
He pressed the intercom on his desk. 'Jane? It's
Gabe. Could you bring in a tray of tea for two
people, please? Thank you.' He came around his
desk, unbuttoning his suit jacket, and settled into
the chair next to her. 'I thought if they didn't know
who you were, they'd leave you alone. I never ex-

pected him to use that protection as some sort of fuel for the fire that surrounds my public life.'

'I guess it's good that they don't know who I am yet, but…what happens if they do find out?' She didn't need that. Didn't need them putting two and two together and looking into her past and dragging up all that history she had. She'd tried to move on from that. This job, coming here, was meant to be a fresh start. She couldn't have it tainted and she most definitely didn't want the papers or gossip mags digging up her past as some sort of entertaining story. Because she'd been hurt. Badly. It wasn't fodder for the masses to dine on.

'I'll protect you. I have lawyers.'

'And have them believing it's something more than it is? It was a work dinner! Can't we just say that? They'll back down, then, won't they?'

'If only it was that easy.'

A knock on his door signalled Jane's arrival. The receptionist came in, placing the tea tray down on Gabe's desk. 'Isla? You all right?'

She pointed at the screen.

'Oh. Yes, I saw that this morning.'

'Could you give us a minute, Jane?'

'Of course.' Jane disappeared from the room, gently closing the door behind her.

'I'm so sorry, Isla.'

'It's not your fault.'

'But it is. They were following me. Looking for a story about me and I gave them one. Making a statement of denial will just continue to fuel the story, I'm afraid. It's usually best in these instances to just say nothing. Do nothing and then they'll move on to someone else, if we don't react.'

'And if they don't?'

'I'd have to speak to my advisors.'

Isla laughed bitterly. 'You have advisors? How the other half lives.'

'What do you mean?'

'That you're used to this. This intrusion into your life. Being seen about town with gorgeous women. That you have PR people, or whatever they're called! I'm just a nurse. Just a person who wants her private life to remain private.'

'So do I.'

'Then why do you court notoriety? Why court all of those women and tease the press? It must work for you, or you wouldn't have continued to do it after the first story.' She didn't mean to say all of this, but she was angry. Angry and scared and afraid to go home.

'I have never pursued notoriety!' Gabe retorted, sounding irritated. 'But this Mack guy is just pursuing some old grudge because my wife, Ellis, chose me, rather than him. And so when I went to a party, after my friends begged me to, I got talking to some young woman, who, yes, was beautiful and, yes, showed interest in me and I had no idea who she was! I didn't know she was famous! But she made me feel a little less lonely, if only just for one night, and after that? Mack never stopped. Once he found out my wife had died, that I was somehow this eligible guy, he went crazy! I never asked for it!'

She looked at him, feeling hurt, feeling bad for them both. They were both victims of a gutter press that looked for anything they considered salacious to sell copies. Even something innocent could be twisted and presented as something else. Something more titillating. Like a new-employee dinner somehow actually being a secret tryst with some new love. 'I can't go home. They'll be waiting for me.'

'You could stay with me, if you need to. I have a big place. There's a set of rooms where the nanny usually stays when Beatrice is home for the six-week break.'

'Live with you? Won't that just feed the fire?'

'They won't find out. The building has private, secure, underground parking, my car has tinted windows. They'd never see you arrive or leave with me.'

'I don't know you. It would be awkward. Strange. We only met yesterday!'

'I know, but if you can't find a place… I'm just trying to protect you.'

'Hasn't worked so far,' she answered, without thinking, then realised how horrible and ungrateful it sounded. 'Sorry.'

'No, it's fine. If you want to make a statement, then I'll agree to it.'

She did not want to make a statement. She did not want to give them any more information about her than they already had. They still didn't know her name, because the ones outside her flat had asked her for it. The flat she was staying at was a friend's. She was renting it until she found herself something more permanent. A place of her own. But if she gave them a statement, she'd have to say who she was and as soon as they got that information... She'd gone back to her maiden name, but someone would surely see through that eventually... 'It would be easier if there wasn't something I didn't want dredging up again. I've tried to move on with my life, Gabriel. This is meant to be my fresh start.'

He frowned. 'Well, how bad is it?'

'It's bad.'

'Your CV was outstanding. I take it it was something private, then?'

She nodded. 'I want to be able to tell you about it, but...if I do, I don't want you making a big deal over it. Not any more.'

Gabriel seemed deep in thought. 'You should only tell me if you feel comfortable doing so.

But I can assure you that I have never betrayed anyone's confidence before and I would not betray yours with anyone else here. Or out there.' He waved vaguely at the window, indicating the outside world.

'I don't want to talk about it here. I just want to get on with my job. Later, maybe.'

'Then *do you* want to stay at mine? The offer is there, until the press presence dies down.'

Isla knew she did not want to have to fight her way through a small skirmish each time she entered or left her home. And Gabe seemed really sincere. He was completely different from how she'd imagined him being. From reading about him in the gossip columns. And he was her employer! Well, one of them. How much time would she have to be alone with him, really? His daughter would be there on weekends, and workdays, she could maybe stay in her room? Lock the door, if she felt she needed to? 'Thank you. I might take you up on that offer. But what about your daughter? Won't she be confused if you have some strange woman stay at yours? Or is she used to it?'

Gabe smiled and shook his head. 'I've never had a strange woman stay at mine. Just nannies, or family members. No celebs. No one-night stands. I'm not that kind of guy.'

'Okay. Thank you. But just for a few days. No more than that.'

'A few days. Till the heat dies down.'

Isla gave a small, nervous laugh. 'I wasn't sure how this conversation was going to go. I'd practised it, but you never can tell how the other person might respond. I wasn't sure I'd still have a job after it, to be honest with you.'

'And lose a brilliant nurse? Never.'

She smiled at him, thankful for his understanding. 'Will everyone who works here say nothing to the press?'

'They never have before. I see no reason why they would now. I trust them. Wholeheartedly. Even Justin.' He smiled.

She nodded, knowing that trust, from her, might take a little longer. But if she was going to live with Gabe for a bit, then she would need to trust him. She hadn't been alone with a guy, for a long time. And now she was going to move into his house, even if it was only temporary. Two days? Three? Surely it would all be over by then?

But, more than anything, she knew she would have to tell him what scared her so much. What she was so afraid the press might find out that would make the story of herself and Gabe sell even more copies. Because Gabe wasn't the only one with a sad and tragic past. She had one, too.

And she'd never ever seen any version of her story in any kind of fairy tale.

CHAPTER FIVE

'THIS WAY.' Gabe opened the door from the parking garage that led to a small foyer that had two options. 'Lift or stairs?' he asked.

Isla eyed the lift and seemed to look wary. 'Stairs, please.'

He nodded and led them up.

There'd been no problem leaving work. There was a private parking area there, too, and at the end of their working day, he'd waited for Isla to be free, catching up on some paperwork, whilst she finished tidying the theatre from the last surgery. Cleaners would come in later this evening, to do the consulting rooms and waiting area. Then, when she was free, he'd walked her to his car and she'd got in, nervously, after placing her holdall in his boot, and he'd driven her home to his place near Hampstead Heath.

He'd already acknowledged to himself that day that what had happened had just been crazy. He'd only met Isla yesterday and yet here he was, inviting her to stay in his home for a day or two, until the press furore died down, but this was the type of life he lived now. He'd not been out to a party or socialising for a while and he'd hoped that maybe Mack had lost interest in him, but clearly not. His fifteen minutes of fame had long surpassed fifteen minutes and he was uniquely sorry that Isla had been drawn into it. He'd thought he was helping, trying to protect her. Trying to shield her. Instead, it had just made everyone think that he cared more for her than he had any other woman that he'd been out with.

Maybe he did?

The other women, they'd been temporary. Women whom he'd known he would only see for that evening. They were dinner companions, dancing partners, but they'd never been anything more than that. They'd been distractions, a way for him to forget how lonely he was and to pretend, even if it was just for an evening, that he wasn't alone. He never brought them home. Nor had he ever gone back to theirs. He wasn't that stupid. Not with the press around. In fact, the press had been an effective excuse for him to not have to date any more. His parents kept telling him that he'd be ready to move on from Ellis one day and maybe marry again, but he'd never believed that. And though the press were a pain, they were also helpful.

Isla, though, wasn't temporary. She was a member of staff. A member of his team and he would have to see her and work with her every day. She did not deserve the intrusion of journalists and their cameras, desperate for some image. And so he'd tried to protect her, believing that he was doing the right, chivalrous thing, and it had only become a nightmare for Isla and he'd felt guilty.

Offering her a safe haven had seemed only the right thing to do.

Unlocking the door to his house, he led her inside. 'Welcome home. Make yourself comfortable.'

'Thank you for this. I won't get in your way. You won't know that I'm here,' she said as she followed him in through the hallway and into the main living space.

He saw her looking around and wondered how she viewed the place. Did she think it homely? Too masculine? He'd picked everything out himself. 'You can make yourself known. It'll be nice to have some company.'

She smiled nervously and he couldn't help but notice the way she clutched her holdall.

'Let me show you your room. You can unpack, take a moment to get settled in and look around. I'll make us both some supper.'

'You don't have to do that.'

'I know, but I want to, even though, I have to

warn you, I'm not a great cook. I once set fire alarms blaring trying to boil an egg.'

Isla smiled. 'Well, maybe I can contribute there. I love to cook. I could cook for us, actually. A way to say thank you for letting me come here.'

He nodded. 'Let's show you your room.'

He led her up the stairs. There were two flights to get to her room, which was up in the attic spaces that had been converted two years ago, so were pretty modern. This was where Janice, the nanny that he usually hired to look after Bea during the six-week break, stayed. It was decorated in a soft grey colour, with white frames, sills and skirting boards. The dresser was a duck-egg-blue to match the bedside units of a double bed, adorned with many pillows and cushions of all textures. A door to the left led to an en suite bathroom with a shower.

'Is this okay?'

Isla nodded, a little dumbfounded. 'Okay? This is bigger than my friend's flat! It's perfect. Thank you.'

'Little bathroom through there, so it's entirely private, and from the window over here...' he wandered over to it and opened the blinds to let in the late evening light '...you can see the heath. It's quite the view.'

'Wow.' She came to stand beside him. Looking out.

He couldn't help but turn to look at her as she gazed outside, her face filled with delight and wonder. He liked seeing that look upon her face. It changed her completely. As if whatever stress and baggage she carried every single day was lightened, even if just for a short time. Her eyes lit up, her cheeks glowed and he saw real happiness there. Real pleasure. All from a view that he took for granted every single day. 'I'll be downstairs. Want a tea or anything? Coffee? Something stronger, now that we're both not at work?'

She turned from the window, the sun creating a soft halo of gold around her head. 'Just tea, thanks. I'll unpack and freshen up, then I'll be down.'

'Take your time. There's no rush.' He didn't want to examine the feelings he was experiencing with her there. They were strange. Unexpected.

He'd not had someone to live with him at the house since Ellis died, apart from his daughter, or their occasional nanny, Janice. But that felt different from this. He knew Isla. Had a work relationship with her. Admittedly it was brand new, but still. It felt incredibly different.

It felt…nice.

Which was odd, because he'd got so used to living alone. Considered himself almost set in his ways. This was only going to be for a few days, but he thought…well, he thought it might be nice, even pleasurable to have her here. Someone to talk to in the evening. Someone to cook with. Someone to share a meal with. Adult company.

His thoughts whorled as he made tea in the kitchen. Part of him telling himself he was being ridiculous, that there was no point reading anything into this. Isla was here because she had to be. Not because she wanted to be. She had been afraid to go home, because she'd been spotted with him. She was probably angry with him on some level, but wouldn't show it, because he was her boss, effectively. She seemed a lovely person, so she wouldn't say it, but he could bet that she felt that way.

Gabe did feel responsible for her being unearthed, but he was determined to make her stay here as comfortable as possible, so that the disruption to her life was as pleasurable as he could make it. And besides, there was something she wanted to share with him. She'd alluded to it at work. Something she didn't want the press to bring back up into her life and though, for the life of him, he couldn't guess at what it was, he hoped it wouldn't cause her any extra distress to bring it up with him.

After about fifteen minutes, he heard her footsteps on the stairs and she came into the kitchen.

'I…er…wasn't expecting guests, obviously, but we need to eat and so I've done a recce of the contents of my fridge and, embarrassingly, it's not much.'

She smiled. 'What do you have?'

'Eggs, milk, a tomato, potatoes and a jar of chillies,' he said. Then, embarrassed at such a short list, added, 'But I do have a full selection of herbs and spices.' He opened a cupboard door. 'A moving-in gift. I've not opened any of them, so they should be good. Or so far out of date that they ought to be labelled a hazardous waste.'

Isla smiled. 'I see. May I?'

He took a step back so she could acquaint herself with the items in his kitchen. Once she'd checked everything, she turned to him. 'Frittata?'

Gabe raised his eyebrows. 'You can make that?'

'Better than that. *We* can make that.' She smiled.

'What do you need me to do?'

She got him to peel potatoes. They didn't need many and, whilst he did that, Isla beat some eggs in a bowl with the chillis, some garlic and lots of black pepper from a pot that had not gone out of date. Not yet. When the potatoes were done, they put them on to par-boil.

'How did you learn to cook?' he asked.

'I used to help my mum when I was little. My dad worked away a lot—he was in the army— so I spent a lot of time with her. You pick some things up that way.'

'You cooked frittata when you were little?'

'No, not frittata. Mum was very much a meat-and-two-veg kind of woman. The most exotic recipe she ever cooked was a spaghetti bolognese and garlic bread. No, I had a lot of time at home a couple of years back and you wouldn't know it, because you work every day, but there are a lot of food and cooking shows on the telly these days. Whole channels devoted to it and I watched a lot.'

'Oh. Okay.'

'The thing that happened, the thing I don't want the press to find out about and bring back up, is the reason I was stuck at home.'

'You don't have to tell me if you don't want to. Not if it's upsetting. I completely respect your right to privacy.'

'I know. But you've offered me your home so that I can have some privacy and in turn I think I should tell you why. You've put yourself out for me and you didn't need to.'

'You don't owe me anything, Isla. It was my fault this happened to you in the first place.'

She smiled. 'Maybe. But I want to tell you. It feels right to tell you. I do want you to know. It will help you understand.'

'Okay. Shall we sit?' He indicated the small dining table that sat in the kitchen.

She felt nervous. Sick almost to tell him. To bring up something she'd sworn she'd never spend time thinking about again. But that had never been a promise she could keep, because the thing that had happened to her had had such knock-on effects on her life that it was with her every day. Every second. She never forgot about it and that was the problem.

'You know I used to work in a hospital as a surgical nurse.'

'Yes.'

'I loved my job there. I had great friends. Great colleagues. We were a family. I worked in A & E for a while, then moved into surgical. I worked in gynaecological surgery. We saw a great deal of cases there. The work was varied. I enjoyed it. One day, we had this patient come onto our ward. A lovely young woman, newly married. She and her husband were very much in love. She came in for a standard hysterectomy. She'd suffered for years with heavy periods and because she'd had two kids and wasn't planning on any more, the doctors agreed to remove her uterus. There were fibroids, all sorts of problems. We said we'd be able to make her life better.'

'Did it?'

'No. The surgery itself seemed to go well. It was afterwards when there were problems. When she came around from the anaesthetic, she seemed woozy, like most people, said a lot of funny things, but seemed fine. It was only when she was properly awake did we realise something had happened. Possibly a stroke. We did a scan and there was a clot in Broca's area.'

'Where we form speech.'

Isla nodded. 'She could talk, but her words were wrong. She mixed up nouns, she forgot names for people and we could see she was in distress. It was too late to use the clot-busting drug, so she had to have another surgery to remove the clot. I sat with her husband whilst it went on. He was terrified. Angry. They'd been told the risks of surgery, but no one ever thinks it will happen to them. He was angry at us and I had to get someone else to sit with him, as I began to feel uncomfortable. Unsafe.'

'Did he threaten you?'

'Not specifically. But I could see something in his eyes and I trusted my gut. We'd advised that the surgery was her best option—removing her uterus—her husband hadn't been so keen. He'd been wary of his wife having surgery. Had wanted her to try other ways to cope with the bleeding and the pain, but she wanted quick results. Permanent results.'

'What happened in her second surgery?'

'The clot was removed and she seemed to cope well with the surgery. But then her bad luck continued and she developed an infection. Her body, overwhelmed, went into sepsis. The doctors tried to get ahead of it, gave her antibiotics, but…she died.'

Gabe sighed. 'I'm so sorry.'

'I'd got to know her and her husband so well. He was devastated. Broken. I've never seen a man so…raw…with grief.'

Gabe swallowed.

Of course, he knew all about grief. She knew that he would understand that part, at least. Just maybe not the part that came next. 'You move on, don't you? As medical staff, you have to. You may have just lost a patient, but there's another patient in the next room and in the one after that and they're still here and they need comforting and support and your professionalism. I had to look after them and I did. It didn't mean I wasn't upset, I wasn't hurting, but it's part of the job. You switch off that part of you so that you can help someone else, and you blow off steam in the staffroom and tell stupid jokes and laugh in the face of such overwhelming upset.'

He nodded. 'It's part of the job.'

'Her husband didn't get that part.'

Gabe frowned now. 'How do you mean?'

'I didn't know, but he saw me. Heard me. Laughing in the staffroom at something and it created in him a rage that…' She swallowed. 'A rage that consumed him. He was waiting for me, in the staff car park, at the end of my shift.'

Gabe stood up straight, looking alarmed.

But she knew she had to go on. Knew she had to tell him the whole thing. She'd come this far, he needed to know. 'He came out of the shadows as I was looking for the keys to my car in my handbag. All I wanted to do was go home and raise a glass to his wife's memory. To shed my tears there. Only he stopped me. Grabbed me.'

Gabe stared. 'What did he do?' he asked quietly.

'He said I hadn't cared. That to me, his wife had just been a piece of meat and that he would treat me the same way. He hit me, with his fist, in my face. I remember falling to the ground, I remember, strangely, the smell of the parking garage—petrol, exhaust fumes, cigarettes—but, thankfully, not much of the attack that followed.'

Gabe rubbed at his face. 'Dear God…'

'He hit me. Kicked me. A lot. Broke four ribs, shattered my jaw. I believe he was going to do more to me. He ripped my uniform open, but I must have begun to scream or something, because people came running. He ran away, but I was able to tell the police who it was and he was arrested, whilst I had surgery to fix my face.'

Isla gave herself a moment to breathe slowly. 'He was put in prison for GBH, but he's out now. Good behaviour.' She smiled wryly. 'He thinks we ruined his life, so he ruined mine. He didn't go after the surgeon because he was a big, tall six-footer of a man, so he came after me because he heard me laughing at a joke. Because I was small. Weaker than him. An easier target for his anger. So, he ruined me. Ruined my marriage. Somehow it came between us. Karl was frustrated that he couldn't protect me, I was angry that he wasn't there when he'd meant to be meeting me after work and we ended up splitting up. It should never have happened, but our relationship had been tense before that anyway, so…it was just the final push it needed to go over the edge.'

'I'm sorry. That's why you don't want the press finding out who you are.' A realisation swept over his face. 'You were *Isla Green*, weren't you? I remember the case in the paper now. Because of your case we ensured our staff had a secure car park. That's why I thought I recognised you.'

'I went back to my maiden name.'

He nodded. 'What happened should never have been allowed to happen. I'm so sorry you had to go through that.'

'Not as sorry as me. It's made me wary of men. Wary of laughing at jokes. Of having fun. It always makes me feel guilty. Like I should never be happy again.'

'You can't let that man's bad choices rule your life.'

'I know, but it's easier said than done.'

The potatoes had begun boiling away at some point, and Isla turned them off and grabbed a strainer to drain off the water. She placed the potatoes on the side and turned to look at him. 'Your security means a lot to me. It's one of the reasons I wanted the job. To get back my career. To start afresh. To begin again. I don't need my past being dredged up. I've already fought so hard to put it behind me.'

He nodded. 'I won't let them bring it up.'

'You can't decide that,' she said softly. But she was grateful for his answer. His determination.

'Maybe not. But I can keep you safe. You need to trust me on that.'

He stood right in front of her now. Close. Too close? Isla smiled gratefully, but backed away. His proximity was too much. Her brain felt too full of thoughts. Ideas. Imaginings with him this close. He was handsome. More handsome than any man had any right to be and this close? That perfection was overwhelming. His blue eyes so bright. His lips so welcoming. His jaw, solid and square. But it was the way he was looking at her, that promise of protection, that he would keep her safe.

It was dizzying.

'Gemma Hargreaves?' His patient sat in the waiting room, looking nervous, her nose clearly bent out of shape, but, surprisingly, sitting next to her was Isla, in her scrubs, and she was holding Gemma's hand. Clearly some connection had already been made. 'Isla can come in too, if you'd like?'

'If that's okay?'

'Of course it is.' He stood back, smiling as they both entered the room and sat down. 'You're here for a rhinoplasty consult, is that correct?'

Gemma nodded. 'Yes, as you can see it's a little out of shape thanks to an ex-boyfriend.'

Isla was holding her hand and now he understood why they had bonded. He examined Gemma, with her permission, talked her through her options, letting her know he would have to rebreak the cartilage in her nose to straighten it. She seemed to flinch at that, but unfortunately it was a necessary part of the process. 'But obviously you will be completely anaesthetised.'

'Will it hurt?'

'It will be uncomfortable, but we can prescribe you some painkillers and give you advice on self-care afterwards, so that we try to make it as painless as possible.'

'Sign me up,' Gemma said simply. 'I'm not going to let what that man did sit on my face for all to see for the rest of my life. It feels like he branded me and I want all traces of him gone.'

Gabe knew that he could fix the physical for Gemma. But the emotional hurt? The mental hurt? That might take longer. When she was gone, he turned to Isla. 'You okay?'

'I felt her pain. I'd brought a discharge form out to Jane on Reception and we were chatting when Gemma came in. She looked so nervous! So I sat next to her and she began to tell me her story and I just knew exactly how she felt. I guess we connected.'

'I'm not surprised.'

'When she spoke about trying to erase the brand he'd left on her...my heart almost broke for her. Do you know that most women are attacked by someone they know? By someone who supposedly loves them? It's a shocking statistic.'

'It must make it hard to trust anyone.'

'I'm always looking over my shoulder, you know? Wondering if he's there. If he still holds a grudge. The victim's justice worker assigned to me said that he'd changed in prison. Accepted his role in what happened and had sought forgiveness from God, but that he'd like to receive forgiveness from me, write me a letter, but I didn't want it. Now I'm terrified he'll find out where I'm living now and visit me, just to say sorry.'

'It's wrong that you should have that hanging over you.' He'd got closer to her, passed her a tissue when he'd seen that she was near tears from it. The man's sentence was over, but it was never going to be over for Isla. He'd wanted to comfort her. Make her see that not all men were like that. That some men were tender. Kind. Considerate. He hoped he'd made Gemma feel the same way. That he could be trusted.

She'd taken the tissue. Dabbed at her eyes with it, then laughed. Gulped. 'Look at me,' she said. 'I should be over this, right? It happened years ago.'

'Two years ago. Not that long.'

She leaned in, rested her head against his arm and the temptation to put his arm around her and pull her close was overpowering in its intensity.

But Isla was vulnerable. Fragile. He didn't want to take advantage. But she'd leaned into him, right? She'd sought comfort from him? So he lifted his arm, draped it around her shoulder, gave her a supportive squeeze to let her know that he cared and that she was safe here with him.

Gabe had never been a victim of crime. He'd never been assaulted. But he'd dealt with patients who had been and he knew trauma like this very often never went away. Victims carried it with them always. Like a shadow. Sometimes unseen.

She sniffed. Dabbed at her eyes and then looked up at him, gratitude in her eyes, thankfulness in her gaze, but something happened in that moment with him standing there, holding her close. Her looking up at him, her eyes glassy with tears of pain and fear.

He wanted to kiss her. Pull her close and take

her in his arms and show her that a real man wasn't about violence, or strength or power. That a real man could respect her. Touch her tenderly. Value her. Admire her. Be wowed by her. And give her exactly what she needed in that moment.

She must have seen the intention in his eyes to kiss her.

Maybe his gaze had dropped to her full, very beautiful lips?

Maybe she'd sensed something in the way that he held her?

That realisation in her eyes, the realisation of his own how afraid she was of him in that moment, cooled his jets and he backed away.

He didn't want her to be afraid of him! He never wanted that from any woman!

'I...er...ought to get back to work,' she said, her cheeks ablaze with red.

'Of course. Yes. Thank you for your...assistance with Gemma. I'm sure she appreciated that very much.'

Isla nodded.

'It's good for people to know they have someone in their corner. I see it all the time when I go to India.' He thought of all the women he treated there. Women who'd had acid thrown in their faces from spurned men. Angry men. The women that turned up alone to his clinic frequently took longer to heal and get over their trauma than those that had support.

'I—I'll see you later.' And Isla slipped from his room.

Gabe sank into his chair when she'd gone, head in his hands. How had he let that happen?

When they got back home that evening, they settled into an awkward routine. Her watching him carefully, assessing him from across the room. He would chatter inanely about anything, keeping their conversations brief, light, uncomplicated. He expected at any moment that she would say that she would leave, go back to her place, but she didn't, because the press still weren't letting it go. They'd released an article guessing at who his mystery woman was and had suggested five women whom it might be.

All wrong, thankfully.

But tonight? Beatrice came home from boarding school. He'd already called her at school. Told her of their guest and why she was there and Bea had seemed fine with it. Happy almost that they would have a buffer.

He had to admit, he struggled when Bea was home. Always feeling as if he couldn't do anything right. That he was somehow letting her down. That he wasn't enough for her. She was twelve years old, but already he felt as if he were dealing with a teenager. She was so much more mature than her years and yet still a child. It was a confusing mix. For her, as well as for him.

Gabe always tried to make their weekends special. They had a week to catch up on, he wanted to spend time with her, yet she often just sat in her room.

Maybe with Isla there, it might somehow be different? Now he'd have two women who would be awkward around him.

He needed to go and pick her up. The boarding school was just outside London and, though he could pay for the school bus to bring her home, he liked to fetch her himself.

'I'll be back in a couple of hours,' he said to Isla as she began bustling in the kitchen. Part of him wanted to stay and be with her. To sit and talk to her and watch her as she cooked as he had this week. It was nice. It was easy. Being with Isla was surprisingly easy if they talked about inconsequential things. He'd not realised how much he missed having someone around the place. But was it Isla he liked, or just having another person? Ellis had cooked for him, too—knowing his inability to even boil an egg correctly without setting the place on fire. He'd loved his wife's cooking. Had loved walking through the door of an evening and having the delicious aromas of whatever she was cooking drift into his nostrils and dazzle his senses. 'What's on the menu tonight?'

'Just a casserole. Some roast potatoes. They'll keep in the oven until you're both back.'

'Well, hopefully, we won't be too bad, but it is London traffic and Friday evening, so...' He shrugged. Sometimes he and Beatrice got stuck in traffic jams for hours. It was never a problem for her. She'd just stick in her EarPods and listen to some music or an audiobook, whereas he'd have to sit there, hands on the wheel, cursing about delays and trying to start conversations only for Bea to not hear him at all.

'I'm looking forward to meeting her. You're sure she won't mind me being here?'

'Are you kidding me? She's going to love having you here. Means she won't have to talk to me!' he joked, even though, technically, he was being serious. He couldn't pinpoint exactly when it was that his relationship with Bea had begun to falter. Her early years, up to the age of four, she'd been wholeheartedly reliant on him and not noticed that she was lacking in the mum department— even if there had been nights where her crying as a baby had been difficult and he'd dreamed of being able to hand her off to someone else, if just for a minute...

Had it been when he'd hired the first nanny?

When he'd sent her to boarding school?

When he'd bought her that bike for Christmas because he'd thought she was ready for one, even though she'd been asking for a keyboard all year? He could have bought both. Money wasn't a factor, but he'd not wanted to spoil her. Not wanted to throw money at her as a substitute for the lack of a maternal figure. He'd tried to raise her right and yet was failing her enormously. He'd even thought of pulling her out of boarding school, sending her to a normal one, just so that she could be at home all the time, but when he'd suggested it to her, she'd looked at him as if he were out of his mind.

'All my friends are there! Why would you do that?' she'd asked.

Well...yelled. She'd even slammed a door or two, as a teenager might have. And the thing was, he'd known that wasn't a solution, even when he'd suggested it. Because he would never have been home in time to look after her when she got back from a school day. He would have had to hire more staff to take care of her. Nurses to make sure she stayed well and did her clearance exercises. She'd probably end up with a better relationship with people he'd hired than she had with him.

So he'd kept her in Hardwicke Boarding School, kept bringing her home each weekend and kept hoping beyond hope that, one weekend, they would have a breakthrough. They would understand one another. That he would somehow get back the daughter he missed so much. The daughter that he and Ellis had dreamed of.

'Do you…want me to come with you? Keep you company on the journey? We can turn the food down really low, or off, if you'd prefer, and reheat when we get back.'

Gabe was grateful for her offer. The gesture that offered to show everything was fine between them. That she was trying to put the near kiss to one side. But he wasn't sure how Bea would react to that. He'd told his daughter that Isla was just a colleague, hiding from the press, because of course Bea had seen the article herself. Her friends always showed her anything that had him in it. So, if he turned up with Isla, she might see something more in it? The way he had, briefly? 'That's very kind of you to offer, but—'

'Of course. It's okay,' Isla interrupted, blushing. 'I understand you'll want some alone time.' She walked away then, into the living room, to make it easy for him to go without her.

It was probably best, anyway. There'd be an awkward tension in the car on the way home, did he really want one going there, too? He and Isla stuck in that small space together? With no escape for either of them if one of them accidentally brought up something they shouldn't?

He had thought about kissing Isla and Isla had

been afraid and he'd hated that. He wasn't someone to be afraid of. And though he knew it was
nothing to do with him, but with her past, it still
didn't make it any better.

One day, it might be. But not right now.

Gabe picked up the car keys from the hook on
the side. 'Back soon!' and he took the stairs down
to the car park.

CHAPTER SIX

ISLA LET OUT a huge breath of relief when she heard the door open and close, Gabe's footsteps retreating down the stairs to the car-park entrance.

Things had been awkward between them ever since he'd looked at her again as though he was going to kiss her. Honestly? She'd thought about kissing him, too, and that was what had terrified her the most. Not *him*. Not him because he was a man. But her own feelings! But she couldn't tell him that. That would make things even more awkward and she needed to hide out here—there was no place else she could go!

Hopefully, when his daughter arrived, it would make things simpler. Beatrice would be a buffer. They could talk to her, if not each other, and it would be nice to spend time with a young kid. She'd not spent any time around young kids for ages. Except her cousin's, but since moving to Hammersmith, she'd hardly seen them and she missed them. Kids were innocent. Kids were honest. They had no ulterior motives. They were funny. They enriched your life.

Isla dreamed of one day having children of her own. It was a dream that she'd always harboured, and when she'd married Karl, she'd thought that that dream was one step closer. They'd wanted to be married a few years and go travelling, though, before they had their babies, and so they'd not started trying, when Isla got attacked. To be fair, she'd not wanted to start trying back then, because she'd known things weren't right between them. They'd argued about simple things and she'd not wanted to start trying for a baby if they couldn't even agree about whose turn it was to do the laundry.

After the attack? Their marriage was even more difficult. The attack became the final blow that broke them apart. And her dreams of family, of babies, drifted away with the winds. Since then, she'd put the idea of having her own children to one side, believing that it could never happen now, because she wasn't sure if she could ever trust a man again to get close.

If you'd asked her months ago if she could envision a situation in a few weeks' time in which she would move into a man's house and live with him, as a guest, knowing that that man was some sort of celebrity surgeon, known for dating lots of beautiful women, she would have said no.

Would have said it was crazy, and yet here she was. Cooking for him. Sitting with him in the evening and watching movies together.

That part? Was lovely, actually. Gabe didn't mind what they watched. He wasn't like Karl, who wanted to watch only action movies, super-hero movies or war movies. Gabe was happy to watch romantic movies with her. Chick-flick movies. Ghost and haunted-house movies, which were her favourites. He'd sit on one couch. She'd be on the other. Each with a bowl of popcorn. And afterwards, they would sit and discuss what they liked, what their best bits were. If they thought certain scenes could have been different or better.

Isla liked that. She'd also liked discussing books with him. Music. But food most of all, showing him recipes she'd found online and trying them out. Getting him to try her sauces as they were cooking, thrilling at his approval when he made all the right noises. She'd only been here a short while, but already she was beginning to feel incredibly at home. Gabe was letting her feel that way. Going out of his way to make her feel welcomed and comfortable, as if he knew what she needed.

Why couldn't it stay as simple as that?

Why couldn't they remain the friends and colleagues they'd been at the start?

Why had she felt attracted to him?

Why had she gazed at his mouth, milliseconds after his gaze had dropped to hers?

She'd thought about it. Thought about it a lot. Gabe might have a reputation as one of London's most eligible bachelors who had wined and dined many beauties in his time, but she also knew him as someone else.

He was kind. Protective. Loyal. A good friend. An excellent doctor and colleague. Intelligent. Easy to talk to. Friendly.

He'd made her feel protected. Secure. Safe. And that took a lot for anyone to do and he had done so in a matter of hours, and now?

It had changed.

Their relationship had changed. In that one moment that he'd held her in his arms.

She had changed.

And that was the most terrifying thing of all.

'Well, here we are. Do go and say hello to our guest before you vanish to your room,' Gabe said, carrying Bea's bags and books into the house.

Bea pulled her EarPods out of her ears. 'What?'

'I said—'

She grinned. 'Joking!' She shrugged off her coat and draped it over the stair banister. It fell to the floor, but she didn't notice as she headed into the kitchen, where he heard light voices and conversation as he grudgingly picked up her coat and put it on the coat rack where it belonged. Then he carried her bags upstairs and put them in her room.

The drive back had been as expected. Awkward. After her initial burst of conversation, where she'd moaned about having to wait *for ever* for him to show up, she'd got into the car and put in her EarPods. He'd ended up putting on the radio in the car, so he at least had something to listen to, as Bea hadn't spoken, except to ask what was for dinner.

'Casserole, I think, and roast potatoes. Isla's cooked.'

'Should taste nice, then.'

That had been it.

He'd yearned to ask her so much more. How her week had been. If she had any homework. What she'd been up to. How her health had been. If she'd done her clearance exercises daily, morning *and* night. But each attempt had not been heard and so he'd given up. He knew that he ought to have motioned to her to take out her EarPods and listen to him. Demand it, as her father, to get her to show him some respect. But they had such a short time with one another and it was already difficult. He didn't want to add any further resentment and so he let it slide, even though he knew it was probably the wrong thing to do.

He stared at the things in her bedroom. He

didn't come in here often, but when he did he always noticed one particular thing. Bea had a photo next to her bed of her mother. The only one that they'd managed to take of Ellis holding Bea, who was only seconds old, before tragedy had struck.

Bea did not have a photo of her dad on her bedside table. He'd often thought of having one framed and putting it in here, to see if she'd notice, to see if she'd keep it out, but he wasn't sure he'd be able to take the rejection if she moved it, placed it in a drawer.

Heading downstairs, he was slightly taken aback to hear laughter coming from the kitchen.

'…and then she laughed so much soup spurted out all over and hit Mrs Midler in the face!' Bea laughed so hard she began to cough. A thick, heavy cough he was used to hearing.

He'd not told Isla about it yet. Maybe he ought to have? Because he could see the look of concern on her face at hearing the cough. But he was so used to keeping Bea's condition out of the public eye—he didn't need Mack making that into a sob story, too, to fit alongside his 'grieving widower' backstory—that was why he'd not brought it up.

Isla looked to him, as if to say, *Do you hear that cough?*

'Bea has cystic fibrosis. That's what you can hear,' he said in a soft voice, hoping that Bea wouldn't be offended by just telling their house guest.

'Oh. Okay.' Isla smiled at Bea. Accepted it and simply moved on, as if she knew not to make a big deal out of it. *Nurses!* 'And what did Mrs Midler do then?' she asked.

Bea beamed. 'She made this weird squeaky noise and ran from the room!' More laughter between them. Clearly they'd hit it off, already. He felt envy hit him square in the solar plexus. Isla and Bea hadn't been together for more than a minute or so and already his daughter had shared more with his house guest than she ever had with him.

'Oh, my!' Isla put on some oven gloves to open the oven and check on the food.

He had to admit, the house had smelt delicious when they'd walked back in. 'Sorry we were late. There was lots of traffic—I hope the food isn't ruined.'

'No, it's fine! I kept it on low. Bea, why don't you go freshen up and I'll start serving, if you're both hungry?'

'Starving!' Bea said, rushing off to use the downstairs bathroom.

Gabe watched her go. When she'd closed the bathroom door and he heard the taps running, he turned back to Isla. 'She likes you.'

Isla smiled. 'I like her. You have a smart and beautiful daughter. You should be proud.'

'I am. Not that she ever lets me show it.' He grimaced and washed his own hands in the kitchen sink.

'You okay?' She came to stand beside him, looking at him curiously.

'Yeah, just…' He searched for the words to explain how he felt about his relationship with his daughter, but Bea came back into the kitchen before he could say anything. He muttered that everything was fine and then began to lay the table. 'Juice, Bea?'

'Apple, please.'

'Coming right up. Isla? What drink would you like with your meal?'

'Juice is good for me, too, thanks.'

The roast potatoes were perfect. Crispy on the outside, fluffy on the inside. The casserole was thick with gravy and overflowing with chunks of beef, carrot, celery, mushroom and onion. It was a hearty meal. Delicious. 'This is amazing,' he said. 'I don't think I've had a casserole since I was little.'

'I've been trying to expand your dad's cooking repertoire the last few days, Bea. Hopefully, I've taught him some things, so that the two of you can eat at home more.'

'Good. Someone ought to have done it. I learn

cooking at school, but so far we've only done basic things—scrambled eggs and jacket potatoes. Though I think next week we're poaching pears!'

'Lovely! Do you ever get to bring home what you cook? I'd love to try your pears, if you do. Maybe your dad could bring them into work, if I'm gone by then.'

'I don't think so. Cooking is on Wednesdays, so... I don't come home till Fridays.' Bea's eyes darkened.

'Oh, that's a shame. Well, maybe if you print the recipe, you could come home and do it?'

'Maybe!' Bea perked up and shovelled in another mouthful of casserole. 'How long do you think you'll be here for? All weekend?'

Isla shrugged and looked at Gabe. 'Whenever it's all died down, I guess. As long as I don't outstay my welcome!' She laughed.

'You'll never do that,' Gabe said, quickly. He wanted her to feel that she could stay as long as she needed. He, for one, was happy to have her stay and it sounded as though Bea wanted her here all weekend, too. And whatever made his daughter happy was fine by him.

More than fine. Honestly? It was so nice to see her smiling.

Isla got up early and decided to go full out on breakfast. Gabe had arranged a food order and allowed her to choose whatever she wanted and, knowing Bea would be back, she'd wanted to put on a nice spread for his daughter. A thank you. To both of them. It had to be difficult to suddenly have a stranger in your home and she appreciated their gesture.

By the time Bea and Gabe came downstairs, she'd cooked bacon, sausages, two types of eggs—scrambled and boiled—toast, warmed up some croissants and *pains au chocolat*, poured juice, brewed coffee and set out two boxes of cereal. 'Ta-dah!' she said as they both arrived in the kitchen.

Bea tried to smile, but then began to cough.

Isla had heard her coughing upstairs. A deep hacking cough that had alerted her to the young girl being awake.

'Bea, you need to do your clearance exercises,' Gabe said.

'I know.' Bea opened up a small cupboard off to the side of the kitchen and removed an oscillation vest. Cystic fibrosis patients used them to help shift the mucus that they needed to clear from their systems every day.

Isla bit her lip. Should she stay out of this? Or help? 'You okay, Bea? Want someone to help you?'

'She doesn't need help. She knows what to do,' Gabe said, picking up a glass of juice and taking a swallow.

Bea stared at him briefly as she coughed some more, then turned to Isla. 'That would be nice, thanks.'

Ah. Isla was being pulled into a battle between father and daughter. She didn't want to cause any more problems than were necessary, but she had offered to help. 'Okay.' She came to sit beside Bea. 'What do you do first?'

'Huff coughing.' Huff coughing, Isla knew, was to help shift this mucus from her lungs. It required a person to take in a breath, hold it and then actively exhale it with a huff, as if you were trying to fog up a pane of glass.

Bea sat up straight and tilted her chin slightly up, mouth open. Then she took a slow and deep breath, her eyes fixed on Isla, who was supporting and encouraging her. Coaching her. Bea held her breath for a couple of seconds, then exhaled it, forcefully in a huff, which caused her to cough more and bring up the mucus.

It was important to shift it from the lungs as the mucus contained bacteria and could make a CF patient extremely ill.

'And again, that's it. You're doing well.'

Isla was aware of Gabe prowling in the kitchen, watching, listening, but saying nothing. She wanted to look at him, check in with him, make sure he wasn't annoyed that she was helping, but watching Bea struggle through her coughing and helping her with tissues to wipe her mouth and nose was more important. She wanted to be present for her. 'That's it. One more.'

After the huffing, Bea said she had to do her clapping. It involved getting into certain positions and having someone slapping along her back to help release any sticky residue. 'Who helps you with that when you're at school?' Isla asked.

'Matron does it.'

'And is she nice?'

'Yeah. Not bad.'

'And your dad does it here?'

'Yeah.'

Gabe stepped forward to assume his role.

'I want you to do it, though,' Bea said.

Isla glanced at Gabe, saw the hurt upon his face. 'Your dad should do it. He knows what he's doing. I don't.'

'He can coach you. Can't you, Dad?'

Gabe paused and Isla saw his jaw muscles clench. 'Sure. No problem.' He began to talk her through the exercises. Stood back, whilst Isla drummed along Bea's back. She tried her best to involve him. 'Like this? Or should I do this?'

He seemed grateful for her questions. Clearly he cared so much about his daughter, but couldn't connect with her. Now all those comments he'd made at work about his weekends being tense made sense. Were Gabe and Bea always like this with one another? What had gone wrong between them?

Bea put on her oscillation vest and sat reading a book, whilst she not so quietly vibrated in a corner, coughing and disposing of her tissues in a special container she had at her side.

'How long does she have to wear that for?' Isla asked Gabe in the kitchen.

'About twenty minutes.'

'And she does this twice a day?'

'Yeah.'

'It must be very difficult, as a father, to watch your daughter go through that?'

Gabe looked at her in surprise, then nodded. 'It is. But it's harder for her. She saw a consultant a few months ago. He told her that she may need a lung transplant in a few years and that hit her hard. It's one thing to do this twice a day, but another to know that, despite it, you still might have to undergo a scary operation to save your life.'

Isla reached out and stroked his arm, without thinking. He'd looked so hurt. So terrified himself. He'd already lost his wife—was he worried about losing his daughter, too? 'You'll get through it. You both will.'

'Will we? You've seen how she is with me. She hates me.'

'She doesn't hate you.'

'No?' He didn't believe her, clearly.

But what could she say right now? She didn't know either of them well enough to know exactly what was going on here. 'It's difficult right now, but it's not too late. This is fixable. You've just got to be willing to try.'

'I'm always trying! But she won't let me in.'

Isla could see unshed tears forming in his eyes and wondered how long this had been going on. She knew herself what it was like to have a father she couldn't reach. She would miss him desperately when he was away, but then when he'd come home, he'd seemed to be a person she just couldn't reach. So she'd stopped trying and had begun to resent his strange presence in the house. It had been like living with a ghost. It had resulted in her, as an adult, going out with a variety of men that were unavailable. It had been a difficult thing to resolve and work on and she didn't want that for Bea, or for Gabe. Their lives were difficult and scary enough.

'What do you normally do each weekend when she's here?'

'Not much. She plays in her room. Listens to music. I work in my office.'

'Then change that. Don't stop trying to reach her, Gabe. She may not act like it, but she *wants* you to reach her. She's floating on a raft, out to sea in stormy waters. She needs the safe harbour of her father.'

'Well, then, what do you suggest I do?'

* * *

Whilst Bea was in the bathroom getting ready after breakfast, Isla and Gabe were standing in his daughter's bedroom doorway, looking in.

'There.'

'What?' Gabe tried to follow Isla's finger. Was she pointing at the wall, or the collection of teddies?

'The K-pop poster on the wall. Does she still like them? Listen to them?'

'Are you kidding me? She listens to them all the time.'

'Excellent!'

'Excellent? Why?'

'Because…' Isla had seen a promotional poster for them last week on the Underground and if she wasn't mistaken… 'Here. Look.' She passed him her phone. 'They're on tour and have a concert in Brixton tonight and tomorrow night.'

'Tomorrow night she'll be on her way back to Hardwicke.'

'So tonight, then.'

'You want me to get tickets? It'll probably be sold out.'

'You don't know unless you try.'

Gabe thought for a moment and led Isla back downstairs to his office. Tapping a few keys on his computer brought up some information. 'Sometimes it's not what you know, but who you know. I met this music promoter a year or so ago and he…yes!' Gabe pointed at the screen. 'He might be able to get us in, if there aren't any tickets left.'

He dialled the number of the box office and, as expected, the concert was sold out. But his music-promoter friend was able to use his clout to let them use his VIP box. 'And that way, no one will see us out together.'

'You want me to come too?' Isla asked in surprise.

'Of course! You think I'm going to suffer through this alone? It was your idea!' He laughed.

Isla smiled. 'You're not meant to be suffering. You're meant to be bonding with your daughter.'

'Isn't that the same thing these days?' He winked and then went to the bottom of the stairs and called up. 'Bea? When you're free can you come here a minute?' Gabe turned back to look at her. 'You think she'll like this?'

'I hope so. I guess we're about to find out,' she replied as they heard footsteps trotting on the stairs. Isla had to admit, she felt a small frisson of excitement herself. She'd never actually been to a music concert ever. And even though she wasn't familiar with the band, or their music, she knew they were hugely popular, so it had to be good, right?

Beatrice appeared in the doorway to her father's study. 'What's up?'

'We're taking you out tonight.'

Bea raised an eyebrow, suspicious. 'Where?' She sounded bored, already. Probably thinking her dad meant to take her to a supermarket or something.

'To see a show,' Gabe answered, smiling.

'I don't want to.'

'Not even when it's these guys?' Gabe turned his computer screen, so that Bea could see who he was talking about.

Her eyes widened in surprise, then she looked up at him. 'You're kidding?'

'Nope. I've got us a private box and, if we have time and it's not too late, we might be able to meet the band privately afterwards.'

'Really?' Bea's voice rose in surprise and awe. 'What time?'

Gabe checked the screen. 'Er…seven p.m. it starts.'

Bea squealed. 'Oh, my God, I've got to tell Jenny!' and she ran upstairs as fast as she could, a mixture of coughs and squeals, feet thundering, into her room to no doubt grab her phone and tell her best friend what she was doing that night.

Isla smiled. 'Well done. The first step in Operation Dad.'

Gabe was beaming. 'I think that's the first

time I've made her smile like that in ages. It's a good feeling. I couldn't have done it without you, though,' he said, gazing at her with soft eyes. Eyes that were glassy with unshed tears.

Isla felt embarrassed under such close scrutiny. 'Of course you could.'

'No. I would never have thought of it. We'd have been two separate souls, in two separate worlds until she became a teenager and ran away or something, because she hates me.'

'Not true. She doesn't hate you.'

Gabe smiled. 'So…it's been a long time since I went to a concert. Think us oldies will need earplugs?'

She laughed. 'If cinemas are anything to go by, then…yes. I think we will!'

CHAPTER SEVEN

THEY WERE LATE leaving the house. Beatrice had tried on so many outfits that she couldn't make up her mind and then, when Gabe thought they could go, she began saying she needed to do something with her hair and put on some make-up.

'Bea, you're twelve, you don't need make-up.'

'But what if we meet Han Lee?'

Han Lee was the lead vocalist of Stride, the K-pop band that had taken the world by storm and the guy that Bea had as wallpaper on her phone.

'I'm sure he'll think you're great. Just as I do,' he'd said.

'But, Da-a-ad!'

He'd negotiated that she could do all of that in the car ride over, but that they must leave right now, or they'd be late and she'd never get to see them at all.

Isla had helped. Promising to sit in the back of the car with Bea and help her get ready.

Gabe was most grateful for Isla's help. It was crazy how his relationship with his daughter had changed so quickly in just *one day* with her around. Since hearing that they would be going to a concert, Bea had been different. Excited. Bouncy. Hadn't sneered at him, or rolled her eyes or any of the hundred usual things she might do if they had a conversation when she came home on a weekend. She'd texted her friends a lot. He'd heard her phone pinging with messages all day and when they'd sat down for lunch midday, she'd been so excited she almost hadn't been able to eat. But she'd sat with them. Chatted with them. Had actually smiled at him and given him a peck on the cheek before she'd gone back up to her room for the afternoon.

'What a difference a day makes,' he'd said to Isla as he'd helped her clear up the dishes.

'Imagine what she'll be like tomorrow,' Isla had replied, grinning.

'I think this might be our best weekend we've ever had.'

'Good. I'm glad.'

'And it's all thanks to you. Pointing me in the right direction. I think I'm so used to being the authoritarian, the teacher, the doctor, the physio, the nagger, that I forget to just be her dad.'

'I get it,' Isla had said. 'She doesn't have a mum and you want her to be brought up to take her illness seriously. You just have to remember that she's more than her diagnosis. The CF is a tiny part of her, as far as she's concerned.'

'Is that what she said to you, when you were both talking quietly, earlier?'

Isla had nodded. 'She thinks you don't see anything else. And I think, if you don't mind me saying, she hates the fact that you hide it from everyone. She thinks you're ashamed of having a sick daughter.'

'I'm not ashamed! I've just been trying to protect her. After losing my wife, I'm so terrified of losing Bea, too, that I crack down on her. Making sure she does everything right. Does her physiotherapy. Does her vest. Eats right. Exercises well. Thinks carefully of how she treats her body. I forget she's twelve. I forget that she just wants to have fun, like her friends, to live her life, but I've got her so tightly wrapped in a bubble that I never take her anywhere in case she gets sick.'

'I get it. I do. But you can't let her live her life like that. Because it isn't a life when you're so controlled by rules and regulations.'

Isla had spoken to him then about her father. His life in the army. Everything had had to be just so. Everything had had to be exact. Folded a certain way. Done at a certain time. So that he'd found it impossible to live his life normally when he'd come home and no one had been able to reach him. Gabe had felt her hurt. Empathised with her bewilderment at not being able to be enough to reach her father and chisel her way through to him. He'd wondered if he'd been doing the same to Bea.

He knew he had to let go of the restrictions he'd put her under. He'd thought he was keeping her safe. Keeping her healthy. But with him, she didn't get to live her life! No wonder she wanted to stay at her school, with her friends. It was where she was most free! At home, she felt trapped with him. A man she didn't understand, couldn't get close to. She must have been very sad indeed and he felt terrible for the way he'd approached his parenting.

So, driving to the concert, hearing Bea and Isla giggling in the back of the car as they listened to Stride through the car speakers was heavenly. It felt incredibly good to know that he was making his daughter smile. To make her happy. And though he worried about all the germs she might be exposed to by going to a music concert that would be closely packed with hundreds of people, he knew he had to let her live and experience the joy of life. Otherwise, what was the point? What was the point of any of it? Isla had been right, but why had he not seen it before?

When they parked up at the concert venue and his daughter emerged from the back of the vehicle, he openly gasped at what Isla had achieved with make-up for his daughter.

When Bea had said she wanted make-up, he'd imagined eyeliner, mascara, lipstick. His daughter trying to look older than her years. But again he'd got her wrong. Misread what she'd actually been trying to tell him. Because what she'd had done instead was that Isla had highlighted Bea's cheekbones, temples and just above her eyebrows with an icy blue colour and, in silver, had drawn on stars and sparkles, which were a motif the band used a lot in their promo. Bea looked amazing. Happy. Joyous.

'What do you think?' Isla asked him.

'I think you look stunning,' he said to his daughter, meaning it.

And Bea spontaneously hugged him, thrilled with his reaction and, shocked, unable to believe it, he took a moment, before lifting his own hands to hug her back, but by then it was too late. She'd let go again and was running off, hurrying them towards the entrance.

Gabe was stunned into silence.

Isla laughed, pulling down her own hat. He didn't think anyone had followed them here, but she was wary of being out and about with him again. Wary of being seen again. He'd noticed her grow more nervous as the day had passed and the time of the concert had got closer.

They showed their passes and were escorted to the VIP box, from which they had an excellent view of the stage. The venue was filled to bursting with people, mostly young girls, pre-teens and teenagers, though Gabe saw one or two adults, no doubt parents who had brought their kids. He felt an affinity with them. Wondered if they felt the same way he did.

On their way in, Bea had convinced him to buy some merch including a light up wand and, now they were in the box, he could see that almost every other person here had bought one, too. The concert had probably paid for itself already with merchandise purchases.

But he had to admit, the place looked great and, though he had to shout to be heard, he was having a good time. When the band came on stage, lights flashing, music thumping, everyone screamed with happiness. Stride looked to be a boy group and, not only were they good singers, but they performed dance routines, too, that he couldn't help but notice that Beatrice was copying as she sang and danced along. She coughed a few times and he was very much aware that normally, at this time of day, they'd be working on her breathing, her PT. Her oscillation vest. Getting her ready for bed.

It wouldn't hurt just this once to be late, would it?

A catchy tune began and he and Isla also began

to dance. Just stepping from side to side, clapping their hands to the beat, smiling, having fun. He couldn't help but smile at Isla. She had given him this. This gift of this most precious time with his daughter. This chance to bond. And it was working out just fine! The VIP box meant Bea could enjoy something like this without him worrying that she might get sick from everyone else. They had a form of privacy. They weren't down in the pit with everyone else. He couldn't help but notice how some of the audience were pressed up tight against the security barriers, dancing, singing, waving banners, or their lit-up wands. In front of them were speakers and a line of burly protection detail for the band, who had their backs to the stage, watching the crowds.

'This is so great!' squealed Bea as they launched into another number. 'This is my favourite!'

She began coughing again and he tried not to freeze in fear, as he usually did when she had a bad coughing session, wondering if this would be the moment something went wrong. If this would be the time she couldn't catch her breath. If this would be the thing that would send her into hospital. It was a fear he lived with constantly and it was exhausting. But it was a burden he would carry, as her father.

'What's happening down there?' Isla grabbed his arm and pointed.

He turned back to look at the girls by the barriers. There seemed to be some sort of commotion. The bodyguards carrying someone over. A young girl. She didn't look conscious as they lowered her to the floor. 'Stay here with Bea,' he said, leaving their VIP box and making his way down the stairs to the main arena. He flashed his ID, told them he was a doctor and that he could help, and they let him through.

The young girl was being carried into a private area, away from the crowds, but he could still hear the throng, still singing, still celebrating. Could still hear the band singing.

'What happened?'

'We think she got crushed a little. Said she couldn't breathe and then she passed out,' said one of the burly guys in a neon-yellow jacket.

'She may have fainted.' He quickly examined her. She was breathing still, but was unconscious and he thought he could see little specks of blood in bubbles around her mouth, so he moved her into the recovery position and checked her pulse as someone arrived with a medical bag and oxygen. 'Thanks.' He attached a mask and tube to the oxygen, then placed the mask carefully over the girl's face. 'Do we know her name?'

Everyone shook their heads.

'Who is she here with?'

'Me! She's here with me. Her name's Lola.'

Gabe turned and saw a man he knew very well. A man whom he had had the displeasure of meeting once or twice before. A gossip columnist. A man who had helped make, not only his, but now Isla's life a misery.

Mack Desveaux.

But he tried to not let that put him off. Mack wasn't the important one here. It was Lola. So he pushed aside the years of irritation he'd felt with this man and focused on his daughter. 'I think she may have fainted. I've put her on oxygen. Any medical history I need to know about at all?'

Mack had rushed to his daughter's side and gripped her hand. 'No. She's perfectly healthy.'

Gabe nodded. Lola's pulse was fine and she was beginning to stir, colour coming back to her cheeks. 'That's it. Just breathe, Lola. You fainted a little.'

The young girl slowly blinked her eyes open, then groaned and winced, looking a little dazed to begin with, then frightened as she realised she'd lost consciousness for a bit. 'I feel sick. I hurt.'

'It's all right, pumpkin. I'm here. Dad's here.' Mack leaned in and kissed her on the forehead.

'Dad!'

'I know, honey. I know. It's okay. This man's a doctor. You're all right now.'

'You feel sick because you fainted, but don't worry, that'll pass.'

Gabe couldn't help but notice how close they were, and even though he disliked Mack immensely for having run a number of stories on Gabe he was hit with a wave of envy for how easy some people's lives were and wondered why his was anything but.

But the blood around her mouth bothered him.

'Is everything okay? Can I help?' Gabe whipped his head around at Isla's voice in the doorway behind him. What were they doing here? He'd told them to stay in the box. But there she stood, hands on Bea's shoulders, in front of her. 'Sorry. But Bea was worried.'

'We need to do a primary survey. There's blood around her mouth,' he said.

Isla stepped forward. 'She was crushed. She may have cracked ribs.' She glanced at Mack. 'Or something else.'

Punctured lungs. That was what she meant, but hadn't wanted to say in front of Mack.

Mack stood up. 'And you are?'

Gabe tried to motion quietly that she shouldn't say anything, but Mack was in the way and Isla couldn't see.

'Isla French. I'm a nurse. Let me help.' She pushed him aside to get to Lola. 'We need to check her chest. Has anyone called for an ambulance?'

'One's on its way,' Mack said.

Gabe asked Lola if it was okay to lift her top and examine her.

The young girl nodded, but began to cry.

Isla knelt beside him. Laid her hand on his. 'Let me.'

Gabe nodded and sat back.

There were marks on Lola's chest, consistent with intense pressure from the barrier. A bruise already forming, just beneath her breasts in a narrow straight line, red and purpling. Isla gently palpated Lola and when the young girl winced, she slowly lowered the girl's top to maintain her dignity. 'Definitely two cracked ribs that I could feel,' she murmured to Gabe. 'Could be more, but she needs an X-ray to confirm. Whether her lungs are damaged from the break is hard to say, but judging by the blood? I don't know. She may have bit her tongue or lips.'

'Lola, can Isla check your mouth?'

The young girl nodded again and reached for her dad's hand. He squeezed it.

They removed the oxygen to check her mouth, but could see no signs of oral damage. Lola might very well have punctured lungs. Maybe even a collapsed lung? She did seem hungry for air. 'I'm going to update the ambulance.' He pulled his phone from his pocket and began to dial.

They drove home in near silence, thinking about how the evening had ended.

Isla sat in the back with Gabe's daughter. Occasionally smiling at Bea, she tried to get her attention, but it was difficult, because after the paramedics had helped that young girl into an ambulance Gabe had pulled her to one side and told her exactly who Lola's father was—Gabe's personal nemesis, Mack.

It would all come out now. She'd be in a gossip column again! Her past. The attack. Everyone would know. Everyone at her new workplace. They would all look at her with sympathy. They would all want to ask questions, when she'd thought she'd put this thing behind her. But most of all? It would reveal her location to the man who had originally attacked her. He would be able to find her and, though she didn't think he was a threat any more, she didn't want him just turning up one day to make an apology.

But the other thing, the thing that had made Gabe mad, was that she'd brought Bea into the room with Mack. He'd done his utmost to keep his daughter out of the spotlight that had focused on him, and she could see from the back seat of the car how stressed he was about all of it. His frown.

The furrow in his brow. The way the muscle in his jaw clenched and unclenched. The way his fists tightened on the steering wheel. How white his knuckles were. How forcefully he changed gears.

In the house, he threw his car keys onto the counter instead of hanging them up on their little hook as he strode into the kitchen, grabbed a glass, filled it with water and then glugged it back, before letting out a massive sigh and leaning against the counters, head bowed.

Isla took Bea upstairs to help her with her coughing and PT, feeling it was probably best to give Gabe some space. She wanted space herself. She wanted to pack her things and run again. But she was sick of running! Sick of hiding who she used to be. Her days here with Gabe and, lately, Bea, had been wonderful and she didn't want to lose that. And though Gabe had felt guilty for pulling her into the spotlight, now she felt guilt for putting that spotlight on herself and Gabe's daughter. She wanted to apologise to him. To tell him she would move out again. Find someplace else.

But first, Bea needed taking care of. She'd been late doing her clearance exercises and it had showed, immediately. As the paramedics had begun to place Lola on a backboard to carry her out to the ambulance, Bea had begun to cough.

Her coughing fit in front of Mack and his daughter had been spectacular.

'Hey, is she okay?' Mack had asked.

'She's fine. Come on, Bea.'

Gabe had tried to usher her from the room.

'She sounds sick.'

'She's not infectious,' Gabe had answered.

'How do you know?'

'It's not Covid, it's CF,' Isla had said, thinking she was being helpful. Putting Mack's mind at rest that *his* daughter, who had just fainted, who had fractured ribs, who might have a punctured lung, would not catch anything from Gabe's daughter.

And in that moment, she had seen Gabe close his eyes in dismay. How could she have not thought? How could she have just blurted it out? It had not been her information to tell.

It took a while to get through Bea's clearance exercises. She was so excited about the concert still, had so enjoyed her special night out, no matter how it had ended. She'd even told Isla how proud she had been to have seen her dad in action. And Isla, too. Seeing how they helped people. She'd never really seen it before.

But Isla had taken a huge misstep and she felt so bad. Especially because Gabe had offered her his home. Had offered her a haven, even though they had barely known one another.

Eventually, Bea fell asleep and Isla slipped from her room and stood at the top of the stairs, anxious about going down them and seeing Gabe and apologising. She knew she ought to be more focused on the fact that she had just told a paparazzi who she was, that she was the mystery woman seen with Gabe the other night and that they would bring up her past and make her live that nightmare all over again, but all she could think of was Gabe. Of how she'd told Mack that his daughter had cystic fibrosis. Of how she'd let *him* down, after the sacrifices he had made for her.

She found him in his office, staring at a blank document, the cursor waiting, blinking silently. 'Hey. How are you doing?' she asked, feeling nervous about his response. Would he answer her? Ignore her?

'I'm all right. You?'

Isla nodded and came further into his room, leaving the door open behind her. 'Despite the ending, Bea had a good time tonight. You made her incredibly happy.'

He seemed to ignore her attempt to begin this positively. 'Is she asleep?'

'Yes. It took a while. She was so excited and then her clearance exercises took some time.'

He nodded, steepling his hands in front of him as he considered his screen.

She wondered what he was working on. 'What are you up to?'

He seemed to think for a while. 'I'm trying to write.'

'Write what?'

'A book. I'm trying to write a book. I've been planning it for some time, got it all laid out. Characters. Setting. Plot. I thought now would be as good a time as any to actually make a start, but now that I've opened up a document, I can't seem to find the words...'

She was surprised. 'Oh. Well, I've heard that some people can get writer's block. Maybe that's what you have?'

'Maybe. Or maybe I'm so wound up right now that it would be impossible for me to write anything!' He let out a heavy sigh. Rubbed his face with his hands.

Isla felt her cheeks colour. Knowing she was the source of his irritation. And she felt fear too. The last man she'd apparently wound up had attacked her. Put her in hospital. Caused her to have surgery and counselling. 'Gabe, I'm sorry! I didn't know who he was! I thought I was helping! I thought...'

The fire in his eyes was incredible and she couldn't look at him. Couldn't bear to see the disappointment, the betrayal, the hurt that she had caused him. She stood up. Knowing she couldn't stay here any more.

'I'll go. I'll leave first thing in the morning.'

'What? No! Why would you leave?' He sounded confused now.

'Because I told Mack about Bea. I betrayed your trust, your daughter's privacy.' She began to head out of his office, but Gabe was fast. Very fast. And before she knew it, he was standing in front of her, blocking the doorway.

Her heart began to pound and she felt herself backing away in fear. 'Please…stop.'

Her bottom lip felt trembly. She looked up at him with such apology.

Gabe looked horrified to see the fear on her face. He backed away. 'I don't want you to leave,' he said softly.

'But I told that guy everything—'

'Isla! Listen to me. I don't want you to leave.'

She braved a proper look at him and saw tenderness in his gaze now. Where had the anger gone? She *had* seen it, hadn't she? Now she was beginning to doubt herself. Recognised herself settling into an old pattern of behaviour, of not being sure if she could read an intention or an emotion in a man's face. 'But, but…you're angry with me and you have every right to be.'

'I'm not angry with *you*,' he insisted.

Confused, she looked up at him. How could he

be angry with himself? He'd not done anything wrong. He'd not blurted out private information to a gossip columnist.

'I'm angry because… I'm angry because it's all *changed*. I was protecting you, I was keeping you safe, and now I can't even do that! It's going to be in Mack's rag tomorrow. Who you are. Your past. And I thought I could stop that and now I can't. Your life is going to be ruined by that man, who, because he has an interest in me, will now want to chase you.'

'That's not your fault.'

'It is. I just feel like…' He groaned. 'Damn it! I just feel like I fail every woman that I care about. I couldn't protect my mum when she went through cancer. I couldn't protect my wife or my daughter from getting sick and now I'm failing you, too.'

'Gabe, you couldn't control any of those things. Your wife passing isn't on you. Bea's cystic fibrosis isn't on you and nor is the situation that I find myself in.'

'But I wanted to protect you. I thought I could keep you safe. You have no idea how much I longed to do just that. Just once, I wanted to win against the battle of life.' Gabe walked away from her and slumped into his chair, head in his hands. 'Bea was an accidental pregnancy. Ellis wasn't ready yet. She wanted to work a bit more. See more of the world. But she fell pregnant and suffered horrendous morning sickness. Every time I heard her in the bathroom, I felt guilty. She spent three days in labour and I felt guilty for every painful contraction she went through that did nothing to progress the birth. She was terrified when they rushed her into surgery for a C-section. Bea's heartbeat was decelerating and not recovering. I thought I might lose them both.'

Isla knelt in front of him, listening to him speak. This was the first time she'd heard him share his pain and she knew it was important to listen. He'd listened to her and though she knew he'd lost his wife, she'd not known the details. Nor had she looked them up on the Internet, figuring that he would tell her when the time was right.

'Bea was small and weak, her lungs weren't great and she needed to be on oxygen, but Ellis got to hold her briefly. We thought, naively, that everything was going to be all right, but then Ellis suddenly lost consciousness and all these alarms went off. I took Bea from her and passed her to the NICU nurse.' Gabe rubbed his hands through his thick dark hair. 'She had an amniotic embolism. It had travelled to her brain, caused a massive stroke. She never woke up. I felt it was my fault. I'd got her pregnant. I'd convinced her to carry on with the pregnancy and then she was dead and my daughter could barely breathe and I felt so incredibly powerless and guilty for it all.'

'It wasn't your fault, Gabe.'

'I knew there was cystic fibrosis in my family,' he replied, looking glum. 'My sister, Sarah, had it. She needed a lung and liver transplant when she was twenty-three. She died from surgical complications.'

Isla's heart broke for him! He had been through so much! 'I'm so sorry.'

'I knew I might be a carrier. We found out, much later, that Ellis had been a carrier, too. We should never have had a child and every time Bea coughs, every time she struggles to breathe, I feel guilt.'

'You can't say that! People that have cystic fibrosis can lead incredibly happy and joyous lives!'

'I'd never seen that. I just remember seeing and hearing suffering all the way through my childhood. And now I see it in Bea. And she won't let me comfort her. She's never let me get close. And now there's you. I got you into this mess, put upheaval into your life as you were looking for stability and I couldn't even keep you safe.'

'Listen to me, Gabe. It's. Not. Your. Fault. None of it, all right? You've got to stop shouldering the blame for everything that goes wrong.'

'I've always felt this way. Even as a child. I try to escape it. When life feels dark, when life feels lonely and terrifying, I go out. Find someone to spend time with, put a smile on my face, no matter how short a time.'

'You're talking about all those female celebrities?'

He nodded, looking embarrassed. 'It's shallow and pathetic, I know. You don't have to tell me. But sometimes they make me feel better. Make me feel less alone. Until I come home, anyway, and the house is empty and the silence screams at me.'

'It's not shallow. You did what you did because it was all you knew how to do. But you're different now. And stop bringing yourself down! Think about all the good things that you are! You care so much about the people around you! You're intelligent, you're kind, empathetic. You go out of your way to accommodate people and even offer them a place to stay. You protect them. You're loyal. A true friend,' she said, placing her hand on his knee to get him to look at her. Because she needed him to know just how much good he'd put into her life. How much she had enjoyed being with him.

'This last week that I've spent with you has actually been some of the happiest days I've had in a very long time. So if you're going to perform an account of your life and you're going to measure your success with people, then you damn well make sure you take that into account, too!'

Gabe looked at her. Smiled. 'You're an amazing person, you know that?'

She blushed. 'I try. Despite everything, I try.'

'This past week has been some of my happiest days, too.'

Isla looked into his very blue eyes and lost herself in them. It was as if they were the only two people in the whole world as they sat together in the dim light of his office, the only light source the screen on his computer. He really was an amazing person and she hoped that he could see that. Wanted him to know just how he'd made her feel. And when he reached out with one hand to stroke her cheek, she felt her breath catch in her throat.

His touch was so soft, so delicate, and in that moment, she wanted more. They were both two lonely souls, who had both been through so much, and surely it was only right that they find comfort in one another? It had been so long since a man had touched her like that. Since a man had touched her at all.

After the attack, she and Karl had allowed a vast chasm to open up between them and after they'd split up, it had been like wandering in the wilderness. Isla had allowed herself to be lost, had preferred to wander alone. After all, it was safer to be that way. To not let any man close, and why would she? She'd doubted her ability to understand just exactly what they were feeling. To wonder if they were seeking comfort, or whether they hid a mean streak of violence that was about to be unleashed on her. Men were physically so much stronger than her. She wasn't a big person. Isla was average. About five feet seven. Light build. Thin, rather than shapely. She'd allowed herself to hide behind her uniform. Behind her baggy scrubs. She'd done nothing in the intervening time since her attack to advertise herself as an attractive woman to men, because she didn't want them to notice her.

But with Gabe? That barrier had come down. Because she knew that he saw her. That he understood her.

And now, as his hand cupped her face and he slid off his chair to kneel opposite her on the floor, his face only inches away from her own, her heart thudded in her chest with sweet anticipation.

Was she ready? She felt ready. She felt safe with him. This moment in time. It felt right. She'd come down those stairs expecting an argument, expecting to have to move out, and instead here they were, staring into each other's eyes, blood pounding so loudly in her ears it was like being back at the concert.

She couldn't help but glance at his lips. His

mouth. Anticipating what it might be like to kiss Gabe. Would he kiss her sweetly? Gently? Would the shadow of stubble make her skin burn when he pressed his lips to hers? What would he taste like?

When had she last been kissed? With tenderness? With love? She couldn't remember and her body yearned for it. Her last touch from a man had been extremely violent and it was taking huge amounts of courage here to just sit and wait and see what would develop.

Gabe moved closer. Slowly. Imperceptibly.

She could feel herself grow hot, her breathing catching in her throat, and she closed her eyes, ultimately in an act of trust and submission, and waited for the press of his lips against her own. And when they did, she let out an involuntary noise. A small noise. Not a groan, not a cry, but a sigh. A sigh because she knew she could trust him to treat her right, to be aware of her past and to know that he must take baby steps with her.

His hand went to the back of her head, his fingertips slipping through her hair and gently holding her to him as their tongues met and she felt her insides melt with desire.

All the pain, all the hurt, all the suffering that she'd kept inside from the attack seemed to release in that moment. It was one thing to be brave and to start again and to put on a mask, but that kind of living was hard. It was exhausting! And lonely, too. But in this moment with Gabe, kissing him, one hand on his chest so she could feel the heat of him, the strength of him, his pounding heart, she let that mask slide and she was just Isla again.

The Isla that she'd kept hidden. The Isla that she'd tried to protect. The Isla that wanted to be normal and to be loved. The Isla that had just tried her best in life. The one who dreamed of a fairy-tale ending. Who'd imagined marriage and children and growing old with someone. For too long, she'd kept that version of herself hidden away, afraid to allow it to bloom, because when she had been that person before? It had all been stripped from her in a single act of violence that had had far too many ripples of consequence.

And yet here she was. Finding tenderness. Finding affection and gentility.

And, my God, he's a good kisser!

At some point, they came up for air. She wasn't sure how long they'd been kissing. Time had seemingly slowed. But when they did, she slowly opened her eyes and gazed into his. She was shocked. Surprised. Moved almost to tears.

He looked deeply into her eyes and she saw a question there.

What do we do now?

Their relationship had changed now, because

of that kiss. Before, he'd been her employer, her boss, her friend and salvation. A co-conspirator. Her haven.

But now? He was something more. That kiss had been a torchlight, a beacon, to announce that they both were attracted to the other. That they both had feelings for the other. So what happened now?

Isla didn't want to rush things. She didn't want to make another mistake. She was so terribly afraid of doing that, and what if they'd ruined things now? What if it was awkward? She needed this sanctuary and what if he expected more?

'Gabe… I think that…'

She didn't know how to say she wanted to apply the brakes. Not without upsetting him. Men, in her experience, always wanted more from her, right?

'We should take it slow,' he said for her. Softly. Understanding.

Reassuring.

He smiled to let her know he knew what she was thinking. Feeling. Afraid of.

'We go at your pace. We have all the time in the world, Isla, to get this right. And I will take every second of it, to make sure that you feel comfortable.'

And she was so relieved. So grateful to him in that moment. That he understood her. That he'd listened to what she'd been through and would have known her hesitation. Isla felt seen. As if she needed to cry, so grateful was she for his reassurance. 'If that's okay?'

Gabe smiled, staring deeply into her eyes. 'Of course it is. There's a lot at stake here.'

And he was right. Because this wasn't all about her, was it? Gabe had his own history. His own reasons to hesitate. This wasn't just about him. He came as a package. He had a daughter, who had needs. Who probably needed a mother, but Gabe, protective over his daughter, would not choose anyone. Nor introduce them to Bea, unless he was sure of them. The man had lost a wife under tragic circumstances and he blamed himself for it all. He would feel hesitant about a relationship, too.

So this was a good thing, that they were both being careful. Both being happy to slow things down.

The kiss was a landmark moment. How they moved forward from that was very important. Part of Isla wanted to run away very fast! A kiss was one thing, but something more? Because when she closed her eyes, she could still feel how it felt to have that man fumble at her clothes, to humiliate her even more. He would have assaulted her in a much more terrifying way if those people had not come into the car park and disturbed him. Trying to imagine Gabe unbuttoning her blouse, or removing her clothes, made her shiver and she wasn't sure if it was in a good way.

But she did know she didn't *want* to be scared any more. She wanted to be brave. She wanted to live life unapologetically. Live loud. Live free. But the fear of getting hurt again ran like an undercurrent beneath everything.

'I'd better say goodnight,' she breathed, staring back into his eyes, wondering whether to kiss him again. Instead, she lifted the hand that had been on his chest and gently stroked his face. Her fingertips feeling every bit of stubble. The solidity of his jaw. The way he leaned into her hand and closed his eyes.

'Goodnight, Isla. Sleep well,' he whispered back, opening those intense blue eyes of his and smiling back at her.

Oh, I'm in deep trouble here.

Would she be able to sleep? Probably not for a very long time.

And if she did?

Her dreams would be full of him.

CHAPTER EIGHT

GABE DID NOT sleep well. He'd lain in bed, his mind full of the events of last night, dreading just what would have been printed about himself and Isla in the gossip rags.

He wasn't one for ordering newspapers or magazines, but he did look at them online to keep up with the headlines and as he sat up in bed and picked up his tablet, about to search for Mack's blog, he noticed he had an email flagged as urgent. He went into his email app and saw the email was from Mack himself and it had an attachment. Frowning, curious, he opened the email.

Gabe,

Just wanted to thank you for last night in looking after my Lola. It was nice to meet your daughter and Isla too. Thought I'd give you an update—Lola did have two fractured ribs but thankfully her lungs were just fine! I don't know what I would have done without you there. So... rest assured, I've called off the crew from watching Isla's place and any exposé of her identity or Bea's condition will never come from me.

You have my respect, my guy.

Mack

He clicked on the attachment. An old stock photograph of him from some awards do, dressed in a tuxedo, but instead of a glaring exposé, which he'd been expecting, there was something else instead.

Gabe Newton—Superhero Doc!

Eligible bachelor and surgeon to the stars, Gabe Newton, went from surgeon to superhero last night at a concert for K-Pop group Stride.

Gabe was attending the concert with his daughter, Beatrice, twelve, when an incident near the stage saw the superhero surgeon leap into action.

Stride had been performing a medley of their latest hits, including such greats as 'Why Don't You See Me?', 'Dark Desires' and their best-selling number-one single 'Clouds', when the audience, mostly filled with young teenage girls and their parents, experienced a surge against the barriers due to one member of the band, Han Lee, deciding to tease the audience by stretching out his hand. This surge resulted in a young girl, nine years of age, getting pushed against the barrier and she fainted.

Security guards pulled the unnamed girl free and removed her to a room for treatment, where they were met by Gabe, who treated her until paramedics arrived. The young girl was taken afterwards to the hospital, as a precaution.

Gabe and his daughter then left the concert venue.

It is understood that the band sent their best wishes to the young girl and gave her a private audience in hospital.

Stride go on to their next concert in Brighton, before beginning their tour of the US. Stride have been touring since last year, performing to sell-out crowds all around the world.

The Brixton venue has assured this columnist that safety procedures will be updated in light of this incident.

Gabe stared at the article. There was no mention of Isla! Mack hadn't used the information he had about him at all!

Wow, the guy has a heart.

All Gabe could think of was that he'd wake up to an exposé article and, with her cover blown, Isla would move out again, and he didn't want that. She was such a breath of fresh air to his life. She was helping him get closer to Bea, but, more than any of that, he wanted her to stay. Even though he knew that was selfish. Isla probably wanted her life to just be normal again. To live in her own place. Not be hiding out somewhere. And Mack had called off the attack dogs outside Isla's place.

That means she can go home.

His feelings in response to that shocked him. The idea that he might be home alone again, without her, without her bubbliness, without her smile, her presence...

I don't want her to go.

How quickly someone could unexpectedly change your life.

Because he believed Mack. The man would not send a message like that, after what Gabe had done for Mack's daughter, and then go back on his word. The man might be a gutter snipe, but he'd always kept his word.

But to tell Isla she could go home? After things had changed so much?

Because there'd also been that kiss...

He felt desire flood him at the thought of it and he had to push it away. At this moment, Isla was still fragile and he didn't want to be responsible for breaking her. He would move slowly. Be guided by her. Be aware of how he spoke to her at the clinic—he didn't want anyone knowing about them. And thanks to Mack they wouldn't have anything to explain. They already knew that first picture was the new employee's dinner. They knew that he'd offered her a place until the furore died down, and last night? She'd simply gone with him to a concert for his daughter. They'd accept that version of events, surely?

Downstairs, he heard movement in the kitchen. Isla was up. She always got up early. He often found her busily beavering away making breakfast for them. How quickly his home life had changed in the past week or so! Dressing, after showering, he made his way downstairs, hoping that things would not be awkward between them after last night's kiss. They would have to act normally for Bea and, besides, he had to drive her back to school this evening. Maybe that car journey would be better than the others?

Isla was putting a tray of something in the oven.

'Morning,' he said softly, glad that he could face her happily and not have to show her an article exposing her.

She turned and smiled at him, blushing slightly. 'Good morning.'

'What are those?' He pointed at the oven.

'Oh, dinner rolls, for later. I thought before Bea goes back to school we could take a picnic somewhere.'

'A picnic? Out in public?'

She nodded, folding a tea towel. 'We could find someplace quiet. Where no one would notice us. I wasn't going to suggest anything, but then I saw Mack's article online and…' she smiled, her face softening in a rosy, happy glow '…he didn't *say* anything about me. Did you see it yet?'

He nodded. 'I did. He emailed it to me. I was just as surprised as you. Perhaps the man isn't the stone-hearted monster I always thought he was.' He knew he needed to tell her that she could go home. That her friend's flat was safe again, even if, selfishly, he wanted her to stay. 'And he said something else, too.'

Isla looked curious. 'What did he say?'

Gabe pulled up the email on his phone and showed it to her, even though he knew she would leave. He watched the expression on her face change from curiosity, to shock, to joy.

'He isn't going to say anything?'

Gabe shook his head. 'No.'

'I don't have to hide out?'

'No.'

'I could go back home?'

'Yes.'

But then he saw something on her face. Something that made him think that she didn't want to leave here, either.

'But I don't mind if you stay. I'd like you to stay.'

'You would?'

He nodded. 'Yes. I mean it doesn't have to be for ever, or anything!' He laughed, nervously. 'But you don't have to leave right away. You could… stay until your birthday, or something. I know Bea would like to celebrate it with you here.'

Now she was nodding, as if she was considering his suggestion, mulling it over in her mind. 'Well, if it's okay with you…then I'd very much like that.'

'It is.' He wanted to reach for her. Pull her into his arms and squeeze her tight, but he didn't want to scare her, either. This had to go at her pace, not his.

'Then that means I don't have to be captive here. We could do something outside London today. Away from any journalists. Where people are less likely to notice us. Make the most of Bea's last day. It'd be nice to make it memorable before she goes back to Hardwicke.'

He smiled at her. So glad she'd agreed to stay. She was so thoughtful. 'Bea's always wanted to go on a picnic.'

'Then it's settled.'

'Great. We can ask her when she comes down.' He poured himself a coffee from the machine. 'Are you sure you're happy to be seen out and about with us? People might think if they saw us picnicking together that we were some sort of family.' He wasn't sure if even he was ready for that and the idea of it made him feel strange. He'd only ever imagined a family with Ellis. Picnicking with his daughter and Isla might be seen as their relationship being somewhat more serious than he'd hoped to convey to everyone at work. He didn't want work to be awkward or rife with gossip.

'I could wear a hat, or large sunglasses. You could wear a baseball cap. Go where no one expects us to be.'

'Sounds like a plan. Sounds like you've done this before.'

'Hidden from everyone?' She managed a wry smile. 'I had to, after the attack. People wanted interviews. Exclusives. My phone rang off the hook constantly and I couldn't bear to stay in the house feeling like a prisoner. So I found ways to hide in plain sight.'

'Such as?'

'I'd walk my parents' dog. People don't notice dog walkers, you sort of blend in. They notice the dog more than you. Or walk around holding a takeout coffee. You look like you belong with one of those.'

'You sound like a spy.'

She laughed. 'Sometimes it felt that way.'

'Well, we don't have a dog we can borrow, so where do you suggest?'

'We'll find a park, or open space. What about Richmond Park? Or there's lots of open space around Hampton Court Palace. We could find a little nook there. Have a picnic, or ice cream.'

Gabe nodded. Sounded good. As he gazed at her, he wondered about her beauty. She seemed totally unaware of it. She never seemed to bother with make-up. She always put her blonde hair up in a bun or ponytail. She had that easy, relaxed beauty. Natural. English rose. Did she not know how beautiful she was?

He'd felt something last night with his lips pressed to hers and his fingers in her hair. He'd felt moved. He'd felt…well, guilty to begin with. Isla was the first woman he had properly kissed like that since Ellis. Yes, he'd been on dates with women. Lots of first dates. But he'd always escorted them safely to their front door, like a proper gentleman, and pecked them on the cheek as a goodbye. Once, maybe twice, he'd kissed them on the lips, but it had always been short, sweet, perfunctory and he'd not felt a thing except sadness.

With Isla last night? It had been different. He'd felt himself awakening, as if he'd been in hibernation for a long, long time and her kiss had begun to warm him. To pull him from the winter he'd been in and back towards spring. Where everything was new and blossoming and full of hope.

He'd become used to being shut down. To working, socialising to order, but he'd never been present in the way he had been last night. It had been a dazzling feeling, to realise that he was still there, beneath the layers of mourning that he'd been smothered in for a long, long time.

It had been many years since Ellis died and he'd been like a monk for all of it. And now that part of him had been awakened, he couldn't help but feel pulled towards Isla.

Maybe when Bea was back at school and they were on their own again, they could explore what they'd begun last night?

Upstairs, he heard coughing. Lots of it. So he got Bea's oscillation vest out of the cupboard and her tissues and waited for her to come downstairs to start her clearance exercises.

'Morning,' she said, as she stumbled blearily into the kitchen, still in her pyjamas, wiping at her eyes with a sleeve.

'Juice or water?' Isla lifted up a bottle of juice and wiggled it at his daughter.

'Juice, please.'

'Sleep well?' Gabe asked, coming in to sit beside Bea at the kitchen table.

'Yeah. I had some really weird dreams, though.'

'Yeah?'

He sat listening to Bea as she told him some weird, convoluted dream about a grizzly bear hunting her at Hardwicke, wondering if Bea realised that this was the first time they'd ever done this. Had a natural conversation where she talked to him as if he was a loving father and not someone that she had to battle with. It was a marvel and he would have talked to her about anything. He got distracted from talking to Isla, wanting to revel in his daughter's attention. When she'd finished and she'd started her huff coughing, he decided to tell her their plans for the day. 'We thought we'd go take a picnic in Richmond Park. What do you think?'

Bea was coughing, wiping her mouth with a tissue. 'A picnic? Really?'

Gabe nodded, smiling, loving the look on his daughter's face.

'Yay!' A huge bout of coughing took hold of her then and Gabe got up to help pat her on the back to clear it, as she seemed to be having difficulty.

'But if you need to rest, maybe we should stay in.'

'No! I wanna…go!' she said, coughing some more.

Gabe looked up at Isla, hoping that she would back him up. Bea's coughing seemed a little worse this morning than the last few days and now he was wondering if he should have taken her to the concert, after all. Nothing was worth ruining his daughter's health. 'Maybe you should rest. You're back at school later. Perhaps it's a bad idea to push you again after last night's excitement.'

'Dad! No. I'm fine. Listen.' And she smiled at him, only doing a little cough, now and then.

'Isla, what do you think?' Gabe asked.

Isla was buttering toast, but she stopped to look up at them both. 'I think that you and Bea need to spend time together, but I also think your chest sounds a little clogged this morning. Why not have the picnic in the back garden instead? We can still make it special. It's a lovely day and you get the best of both worlds. We'll have games and everything, but if your chest is bad, we've got everything here to respond to it. What do you say?'

Bea seemed to consider it, but another bout of heavy coughing, where she struggled to breathe, seemed to decide it for her. 'Okay. Picnic in the back garden. But I get to choose the music.'

'Deal,' Gabe said, reaching out to shake his daughter's hand.

Mack's article had surprised her. She'd thought she would wake this morning and see her name and history splashed across his gossip column, but he had omitted her *completely*, instead focusing on the fact that Gabe had taken care of Mack's daughter. She'd thought that this morning, with her cover blown, she'd have no more reason to stay here at Gabe's and she'd have to return to her friend's flat and face it out all over again.

But that hadn't happened and the realisation that she could stay at Gabe's a bit longer? Had pleased her. Especially after last night's kiss. It was as if their little bubble remained intact. Their little secret. This attraction that had been building was still theirs alone. It was nice to have a secret. It was nice to feel this way. When last had she felt this frisson of excitement for a man?

When she'd first met Karl? No. Not even then. She and Karl had been friends first. Colleagues first. What had built between them had been comfortable. Easy. They'd shared a drunken kiss at a work's do and had somehow begun a relationship that way. And though she'd liked him a lot, there'd not been the excitement that she felt with Gabe.

She'd often wondered, as she did now, if she'd fallen for Karl because he was the exact opposite of her absent father. Karl was ever present. He was steady. Sure. Never let her down and encouraged her at work to go for promotion. When she came home, he was always there. They ate meals together. Went out together. He listened to her.

But had it ever been enough? She'd often felt as if something was missing, but could never pinpoint what, but now, with Gabe, she wondered if it was down to attraction. Desire. Karl had been comfortable. Sex with him had been nice, but had it ever blown her world? Looking at Gabe, she somehow imagined that intimacy with him would be…

I can't think about that.

The idea of her exposing herself to him like that. Submitting to him like that. Being vulnerable. It almost seemed too much. When she was attacked, that man who went from beating on her to ripping at her clothes made her feel vulnerable and she couldn't imagine ever being so passionate with Gabe that he'd be able to ravish her with passion, without her freaking out.

I'm not fixed yet. Maybe I'll never be?

When Bea disappeared upstairs to get dressed for the day and washed, Gabe cleared up the table and as he passed her in the kitchen, he brushed his hand against hers.

Heat raced up her arm and caused goosebumps to break out over her skin and she smiled to herself. A picnic here in the privacy of their own garden would be nice. Making food for it would be nice. Playing games and laughing with Bea and Gabe would be nice. Like pretending she had a family of her own, only without all the responsibilities and realities of one. She never did anything like this when she was a child. She couldn't remember any family activities, to be honest.

When the water began to run in the bathroom

above as Bea washed, Gabe came to stand behind her and she could feel his presence, close in proximity. What was he doing? Isla turned slightly and he was inhaling the scent of her hair.

'What are you doing?' she asked, smiling, knowing exactly what he was doing.

'Just…being present. Enjoying that you're here.'

She laughed, nervously. But, despite her nervousness, was enjoying it, too. Was she brave enough to turn around and face him? See what happened? In a moment of crazy courage, Isla turned to face him, smiling, one eyebrow raised.

Gabe stepped closer, smiling back. One hand went either side of her at the kitchen units and, though he had penned her in, she was not afraid. Because it was Gabe. And he was safe. He excited her. He was not a threat. Not yet, anyway.

He leaned in. Came closer. His mouth so close to hers, their noses brushing, teasing her with the idea of a kiss, but not actually kissing her.

It was almost more than she could bear. Her insides were a tumult, her stomach was flipping, her blood was pulsing and her breathing had become erratic, but, despite all of that, she smiled. Laughed.

And the Eskimo kiss became a soft, gentle, real one.

CHAPTER NINE

'OKAY, LADIES AND GENTLEMEN, let's just go through our pre-operative checks. Patient is confirmed as Laurence Haworth and he is here for a deep plane facelift. Date of birth is July twelfth, 1984, so forty years of age.'

Isla checked the paperwork and then the label on the patient's wrist to confirm. 'All present and correct.'

He nodded and checked with the anaesthetist that they were happy to proceed.

'Patient is fully sedated,' he agreed. 'BP riding steady at one twenty-two over eighty-one. Pulse at seventy-one beats per minute and oxygen saturations at normal levels.'

'Then let's get started.'

Gabe was feeling optimistic. Bright. For the first time in years, he'd had a good weekend with his daughter. They'd got closer. He'd felt as though she was finally allowing him to love her and show that love, without considering everything he said as an attack.

It was all down to Isla. She was who he had to thank for this. Yesterday, they'd had a lovely picnic in the back garden together and then they'd all driven together to take Bea back to Hardwicke Boarding School.

It had been nice. And surprisingly frightening how easy it was to imagine them as a family.

'I spy with my little eye, something beginning with B.'

They'd played I Spy in the back garden as they ate their picnic and Bea had been winning.

'You can't keep picking things beginning with B,' Gabe had said, joking.

'It's my turn. I can pick whatever letter I like. Come on! B!'

'Bumblebee?' Isla had guessed.

'Nope.'

'Brickwork?' Gabe had guessed.

'Nope.'

'Beautiful young lady?'

'No!' Bea had chuckled.

Gabe had grabbed at a daisy from the lawn and passed it to his daughter, who had laughed, taken the flower and tucked it behind her ear.

Then she had plucked it back out. *'But this is close!'*

'So, it's a flower?'

'I'm not telling!' Bea had laughed.

'Bluebell?'

'No.'

'Begonia?'

'I don't even know what that is, Dad!'

Bea had collapsed laughing, which had become another coughing bout, and he'd had to pat her on the back to help clear it.

'Butterfly bush?'

'Ooh! So close!'

'Buttercup?' he'd guessed.

'Yes!'

Bea had raised her hand for a high-five, which he'd met with his own, and then she'd instantaneously reached for him to give him a congratulatory hug.

He'd been so startled, so surprised. Bea had never initiated physical contact with him before. Their arguments with one another, their frequent misunderstandings, had kept them apart for a long time. So to be holding her, hugging her, at her desire, had meant so much and almost brought a tear to his eye.

Isla had noticed, of course.

He'd caught her looking at him afterwards, as he'd pretended to think of a letter for his turn in the I Spy game, and she'd smiled happily for him.

He'd been happy, too.

And then, driving Bea back to Hardwicke, they'd arrived at the private school, parked up, got out her things and walked Bea up to her dorm.

Normally when he did this, he would awkwardly say goodbye and then leave, as Bea had made it quite clear she didn't want him embarrassing her in front of her friends. But this time, she'd given them both a huge hug and a squeeze and had happily waved them goodbye from her window.

Gabe had left her behind for the first time looking forward to when he could collect her again. Now he couldn't wait for Friday evening, so he could pick her up again and they could continue growing their bond.

'So, I'm working below the superficial muscular aponeurotic system because this allows me to create tension at the level of the fascia, which in turn allows for a tension-free skin closure for better results,' he explained to Isla.

'I see.' She sounded fascinated and he loved that she was so interested in his work.

'Suture, please.'

She passed it over and he tied his knot.

'Cut.'

Isla snipped it with scissors.

'The patient does have some jowling, and he's asked me to address this too, so could I ask you to apply pressure here on the buccal fat pad?'

Isla let him guide her to place her fingers.

'Perfect. I'm going to make a small incision here.' He made a small incision in the overlying fascia and then began to tease out some of the buccal fat. 'Bipolar cautery, please.' He made sure to avoid injury to the facial nerve. 'That's it. Four zero nylon, please.'

They worked well together. They were efficient and the operation was running smoothly. Isla was an excellent theatre nurse. Gabe couldn't help but look up and smile at her as they worked, and he was about to thank everyone for their assistance when suddenly the machines monitoring Mr Haworth suddenly started blaring alert noises as his pressure dropped and his heart rate went into ventricular tachycardia.

'Oxygen saturations are dropping!' said the anaesthetist.

'Increase the oxygen,' he ordered. 'We may have to cardiovert if this keeps up. Isla? Get the pads ready, please.'

Isla grabbed the defibrillator and opened Mr Haworth's gown to place the chest pads in case they needed to shock the patient.

'One sixty-two BPM,' advised the anaesthetist. 'One-seventy.'

Alarms were blaring.

'Do you think he's having malignant hyperthermia?' Isla asked.

'Possibly. Let's take him off anaesthesia, please.'

'He's in ventricular fibrillation!'

Ventricular fibrillation was dangerous. Life-threatening and needed immediate treatment to stop the patient from going into cardiac arrest. 'We need to shock him back into regular rhythm. Clear!'

Isla punched the button and Mr Haworth's body jerked in response to the shock. 'Still in arrhythmia.'

'Beginning CPR.' Gabe began to do chest compressions. It had been a long time since he'd had to do anything like this, but he was glad to observe, as if from a distance, that he and his team, including Isla, remained calm. They knew what to do. Isla used to work in A & E. She was a good nurse. 'And clear!' He shocked the patient again.

Mr Haworth's heart returned to a regular rhythm again.

They all breathed a sigh of relief. 'Thank the stars. Okay, let's get him bandaged up and taken to the high-dependency ward. I want fifteen-minute obs on him. If you could apply the antibiotic ointment and apply the pressure dressing before he goes up?'

Isla nodded. 'Of course. Well done.'

'I think Mr Haworth will be very pleased with his results. Once he gets over the shock.'

'So do I.'

Her eyes gleamed with happiness over her surgical mask and he felt the urge to go over to her, pull that mask down and kiss her now that the adrenaline was not coursing through his body.

But they were at work and he couldn't do that, so he tried to keep his tone brisk as he thanked everyone in the room for their assistance and then left Theatre to scrub out.

As he washed his hands, he wondered how long he and Isla would be able to hide their feelings for one another at work. At home, it was easier. Especially now that Bea was back at school, too. Since their kiss, it was all he could do to not think about her. He wanted more, but he knew he had to move slowly. Kissing her was amazing. So amazing, he'd begun to wonder what it might feel like to do other things to her, but he didn't want to scare her off. She'd been through a trauma. He would have to be guided by her, when she was ready for more.

But by God, he wanted more! Moments like this showed him that life was short and could be taken from you unexpectedly.

'We've placed you in a compression bandage, Mr Haworth. You'll need to wear it for at least the first twenty-four hours continuously. This is to minimise swelling and ecchymosis.'

'What the hell is ecchy…eccthee…?'

'Ecchymosis?' She smiled at her patient. 'It simply means bruising.'

'Then why don't you say bruising?'

She smiled. 'Sorry. We medics have our own

terms for things and we get used to them, forgetting that not everyone knows what they are. You'll need to keep your head elevated for about the first week, so sleep on lots of pillows. And, as explained before, no rigorous or physical activity for two weeks.'

'Okay. Should be doable. But the big doc here is looking at me as if something bad happened. Should I be worried?'

Gabe smiled. 'As far as your cosmetic surgery is concerned everything went very well, Mr Haworth, but the surgery did present with a complication. You went into an arrhythmia and we needed to shock you and do CPR. Now this could simply be because your body was too tired from the anaesthesia, but it could also imply that there may be a weakness with your cardiac system and I would like to refer you for further testing, just to make sure that you're okay and that there's nothing wrong with your heart.'

'There might be something wrong with my ticker?'

'We won't know for sure. Your pre-surgical tests did not show anything at all worrying, so I'm hoping it was nothing more than your body growing tired from the procedure, but let's get you referred and checked out just to be sure, okay?'

Mr Haworth nodded.

'I'll refer you to Mr West. He's the best in the business and he'll be able to see you soon.'

'Thanks, Doc.'

Gabe smiled. 'And now I'll leave you in Nurse French's very capable hands.'

When Gabe had gone, Isla turned back to her patient. 'Tomorrow we'll check your drain and do the dressing removal.'

'Yes, miss.'

She smiled at him. 'We'll make appointments to see you again in four days and seven days to assess the wound. But you have our details—any problems or questions, don't hesitate to ring us.'

'Will do.'

'You have someone to look after you when we let you home?'

Laurence nodded. 'My wife.'

'Is she coming later?'

'She should be here any minute. She wasn't a fan of me getting the surgery. She said I looked just fine as I was. But I didn't feel fine. I don't think I've aged well. Lots of stress at work and all that, which might explain the old ticker, too, but my wife still looks like she did when she was twenty. Everywhere we go other guys would be eyeing her up and assuming I was her dad or something.'

'Surely not?'

'I'm telling you the truth. I just wanted to feel

youthful again. Recapture that spirit of confidence of looking in the mirror again. To stand by my wife's side with pride. Now I've got to worry about something else.'

'I'm sure she's very proud to stand by you. And try to look at this as being fortunate. You've been given a warning. A chance to do something about it and take action.'

Laurence tried to grin. 'I do like your spin. You ought to have gone into politics, miss!' He laid his head back against the pillows and closed his eyes.

Isla left him to rest. Though patients often went home within a few hours of the surgery, they liked to monitor them first, check their observations and make sure there were no complications after their surgery and anaesthetic. And patients like Mr Haworth needed extra stays. Extra monitoring.

As always, she'd been thrilled to watch Gabe work, and seeing him cope with the emergency? She'd been very proud of the way he smoothly went from calm and controlled to reacting fast and thinking on his feet and keeping control of the situation. She enjoyed assisting all of the partners in the Garland Clinic, but Gabe especially. When she saw his name on the board, she'd look forward to it all day, getting to spend that extra time with him, even though she shared his home, too. He was an exquisite surgeon. Polite. He didn't have a God complex. He wasn't arrogant, as she'd thought he might be, before she began working here. He was an educator. Kind. Funny.

Surgeries were done for the day and they were getting ready to go home. She knocked on his office door, before going in. 'Hi. You ready?'

'Just a sec. I need to send an email.'

She stepped over to his bookcase and perused the titles whilst she waited. Behind her, she heard the sounds of his keyboard as he typed and she realised she was so looking forward to getting home and cooking for him and...what? This was their first night alone in the house since Bea went back to Hardwicke. Would they kiss again? Snuggle on the couch? Or would he want more?

Isla glanced at him.

His brow was furrowed, his lips moved slightly as he spoke the words to himself as he typed. He was such a handsome man and when she looked at him, she felt for him, for all the pain that he'd been through. They'd both experienced trauma. His wife had died, unexpectedly and tragically. He'd been left to look after a daughter that had struggled to breathe. He'd been alone all this time.

Was he lonely? Was he looking for someone who could give him a commitment? Not just him, but his daughter, also? Or was he afraid of getting hurt again?

What did Gabe see when he looked at her? Someone he could have fun with? Or something else?

It was the something else that worried her. Though she craved a family of her own, to one day hold a baby of her own, she feared the steps she would have to go through first.

It was so strange to desire intimacy and yet be so terrified of yielding to it at the same time. When people were hurt, you helped heal them by hugging them. By showing them that you loved them. It was never just words. It was acts of love, too. But what was a person to do when that very act scared the living daylights out of you?

She had no doubt that Gabe would be tender and kind. But that didn't help any when she still suffered the occasional flashback. When she saw the face of her attacker lunge close as he decided he wanted more than to just beat her... His eyes... his face...the spittle. The things he'd said, the names he'd called her, as he'd torn at her uniform.

Isla swallowed and closed her eyes, dismissing the images, banning them once again and forcing them to the back of her mind.

She couldn't ever imagine Gabe being rough, or scaring her. But she needed to be brave enough to let him try.

Could she do that?

Was there a way?

Maybe I need hypnotherapy or something.

Because if she were to ever be intimate with Gabe, she'd want to enjoy it. All of it. Every moment. Not be fighting flashbacks. Gabe was such a special person, he deserved someone who would enjoy his every touch. Who would shiver with delight, not fear, at his fingers caressing their skin. Who would close their eyes and sigh with pleasure and revel in the moment.

I deserve to be able to feel that way when he touches me.

She'd not heard him switch off his computer, or get up from his desk, so when he was suddenly behind her, his hand on her arm, she jumped.

'Sorry.'

'No. It's okay. I was just lost in my own daydreams there.' She smiled at him, not wanting him to feel guilty for something that was not his fault.

'Ready to go home?' he asked softly, smiling at her with such tenderness.

'Yes. Absolutely.'

CHAPTER TEN

She'd sat in the car with him on the way home and they'd enjoyed a pleasant journey, her stomach grumbling with hunger because she was starving. She was determined to cook something nice when they got back.

'What are you doing?' Isla looked at Gabe with a smile upon her face.

They'd got home quite quickly and she'd told him she was going to cook a mango curry and asked could he get the red curry paste from the fridge. Talking about whatever it was might be easier whilst they were cooking.

'It doesn't seem to be here.'

She laughed. 'In the door, second shelf down, right next to the sweet onion chutney.'

'Aha! Got it. Thanks. I could have sworn it wasn't there a moment ago.'

'How are you a world-class surgeon, who can see two nerve endings that need to be spliced together, but you can't see a red jar that's right in front of you?' She laughed again as she stood at the counter chopping courgette and yellow peppers.

'Because I'm a man. Genetically programmed to not see what's right in front of me when I'm looking for it.'

'Right. Okay. Do you think you could go in the pantry and see if you're able to find me some shallots?'

'I don't know, let me try.' He passed her the jar of curry paste, then went to the pantry, opened it up and rummaged in the onion bag. 'How many?'

'Three or four should do it.'

'Coming right up.'

She loved cooking with him. It was the shared activity of it, the camaraderie, the fact that though Gabe could do all manner of expert things in a surgical theatre, his skills in a kitchen were less so. He'd burned sausages the other day. He'd said it was because he'd got distracted, found things to do whilst food was cooking and then forgot he was cooking, until the smoke alarm had reminded him rather loudly. But he did like cooking with her and she liked the fact that, in the kitchen, the boot was on the other foot. At work, Gabe taught her, educated her, tested her knowledge and skills, and yet in the culinary arts, she was the teacher and he the pupil.

It was nice. Karl had never been interested in cooking. He liked the end result, but he never wanted to cook. He'd always let her do it and so she'd spent many hours in the kitchen alone. Having Gabe with her, helping, telling her stories about his day, or his life, or sharing jokes with her? It was so special. So delightful. She knew she'd miss it incredibly when she finally returned home.

Because that would happen at some point, right? She'd have to go home at some point. She couldn't stay here for ever—he'd invited her as a temporary thing. But she loved that they could cook and share car journeys and in-jokes with one another and, at the end of the day, Gabe would kiss her goodnight.

It was going to be her birthday soon. It would fall on a weekend, when Bea would be back, and she was so looking forward to it. Having a birthday as part of something special.

Isla hummed to the music playing on the radio as she placed the chopped shallots in a pan, with a little oil, and began to fry them, adding a spoonful of garlic paste as the onions began to cook. Was there any better smell in the world than that? 'Can you pass me the courgette and peppers, please, before you eat them all?' She smiled at him as he passed her over the dish with the chopped vegetables.

'You know you're bossy in the kitchen?'

'Am I?'

'Yes. But I like it. It's assured. It's confident. And I like to dine on food that's been cooked by a confident chef, who knows food and has a refined palate.'

'I'm not sure I have a refined palate, but I'll take the compliment.'

'You didn't ever think about becoming a chef?' he asked.

'Not really. I think I always wanted to be a nurse. Didn't you always want to be a doctor?'

'Actually, no. I always thought that I'd be a K9 police officer growing up.'

'Really?' She looked at him in surprise. 'What stopped you?'

'Dog allergy.'

'You're kidding?'

'Nope. I break out in hives. So I looked to become something else. I'd always been interested in medicine, too, and decided to become a GP. But then, during placements in training, I discovered a love for surgery and here we are.'

'Oh.'

'What?'

'Nothing. It's just that…when I think of my future…of what it might look like when I settle down and hopefully have a family of my own, I've always imagined I'd have a dog. I don't know what I'd do if I ever found out I was allergic.'

'You could take antihistamines.'

'Or get a dog that's allergy friendly. There must be some, right?'

'Well, let's see.' Gabe got out his phone and began scrolling for information as Isla added ginger and the red curry paste to the softening vegetables. This was most definitely procrastination and it worried her. 'Here we go! You can have a Yorkshire terrier. Apparently they have hair, rather than fur, so they're hypoallergenic.'

'Great. You could get yourself a terrier, too.'

'I've always pictured myself with a German shepherd. I'm not sure a Yorkie is my jam.'

'I'm sure you'd find them adorable if you got to know them.'

'I guess. I could train it to be a guard dog, too, right?'

She laughed. 'Absolutely! Why not? People need ankles.'

The DJ on the radio suddenly began to play a song that Isla hadn't heard in ages. It took her back to her teenage years. To hearing it and dancing to it at her first ever party.

'Oh, I love this song!' She began to sway.

'Then dance with me.' Gabe turned down the hob and then took Isla's hand and led her out into the centre of the kitchen and pulled her into his arms.

She couldn't help but laugh. Blush a little. Dancing in the kitchen. Pressed up close. She thought that maybe they'd sway together for a little bit, he'd twirl her around a few times and then they'd go back to cooking.

Only that didn't happen.

He held one of her hands close against his chest. With the other he led and she was pressed up close to him. Very close. They'd kissed before, their lips might have met, but she'd never felt the length of him pressed up against her like this.

Isla felt herself grow hot. A heat of awareness, of desire, of apprehension washed over her. She did not know what was going to happen and that was not a feeling that she was comfortable with.

Since the attack, Isla had controlled every aspect of her life. Who she allowed to get close. Who she allowed herself to get attached to. Friends. Colleagues. Family. Romantic attachments had never been allowed as she'd always been afraid of letting anyone close, because as soon as someone invaded her close personal space, she often felt herself freaking out and so it had just been easier, the last year or so, to keep everyone at arm's length.

And now she found herself in Gabe's arms, marvelling at the way his thumb was stroking her hand against his chest, the way his beautiful blue eyes were gazing at her.

I want this. I want this all the time.

Her heart thudded in her chest. Her mouth

went dry and she had to fight the urge to break away. Her brain screamed at her to break it off, to go back to cooking, to where the situation was friendly and warm and safe, but her heart, her body, which had been starved of love and comfort and gentle touch, wanted her to stay exactly where she was.

It was dizzying. Confusing.

Which voice to listen to?

He wasn't doing anything threatening. He wasn't being rough. He was being kind. Gentle. And now he'd laid his head against hers and they moved to the music and she closed her eyes and told herself to just focus on that. The movement. The rhythm. The normality. It was just a dance. He wasn't trying to feel her up. He wasn't trying to remove her clothes. They were just dancing. And this song wouldn't last for ever, so…

Just enjoy it.

And so she tried. Maybe ninety per cent of her tried. The rest? Was on full alert. Waiting for something bad to happen. Because something always did.

Panic washed over her in a wave.

'I haven't danced like this in ages,' Gabe said, softly.

'No?'

'I never danced any slow songs with anyone. Not like this.'

'Oh.' She wondered if he was struggling with the moment, too? If he'd not danced with anyone at parties like this, was his last slow dance with his wife? 'You must miss Ellis, so much.'

He stopped dancing. Pulled back to look at her. 'Of course. I will always miss her. She was taken from me before her time.'

It was as if a wall came down between them, and they separated. 'I didn't mean to imply that you were dancing with me like that because you missed her. I was just thinking who you must have last slow-danced with.'

His eyes had darkened. 'It was with Ellis. We danced the night before she went into labour with Beatrice. I stood behind her and danced because her baby bump was so big.' He swallowed.

'I'm sorry you lost her like that. Truly.'

He nodded. 'I've been trying to move on. Sometimes I forget her. I can go a whole day and not think about her and then, when I remember, I feel so guilty. Holding you in my arms and hearing her name at the same time made me feel...' He didn't say guilty.

But she knew that was what he meant.

She had made him feel bad and she hadn't meant to. They'd been having a moment and she'd spoiled it. But had she done so deliberately? The song had been coming to an end and she'd been worrying about what would come next. If they'd carried on dancing, holding each other close, would it have progressed to something more? Because she'd been scared of that. Had she self-sabotaged the moment? And if so, what did that mean?

That she wasn't ready for intimacy?

And clearly, Gabe still had a hang-up about his wife.

'I'll carry on with dinner. Why don't you get a glass of wine?' She realised she'd said something a wife might.

You relax, honey... I'll cook dinner.

Maybe she ought to rethink this living arrangement? Maybe she ought to go back home? Clearly this thing between her and Gabe was reaching a turning point that she wasn't sure either of them were ready for.

She couldn't handle intimacy. He was still missing his wife.

But the truth was, she'd begun to like it here. She'd begun to feel settled. Going to bed at night, knowing that Gabe was near, like a security blanket. Living in her perfect, comfortable home. Driving into work with him, driving home with him. It was all very domesticated. And Bea? She loved Bea. She was a wonderful young woman and they got along great.

What would her life return to if she gave all of that up?

Would it be as empty as it was before?

Would she feel as alone as she had?

And how would Gabe take her leaving? Because he seemed to like having her here.

She would be leaving because of herself. Because she was afraid of what it would mean for them if she stayed. Because the truth was—she could feel her feelings for Gabe were growing. Exponentially. It was why she had allowed him to get so close. It was why they had kissed. It was why she had allowed him to pull her close for that dance.

But fear was an insidious thing.

It crept into the cracks of a person's armour and took hold.

Isla just had to decide whether she wanted to live in fear of the past, or step boldly and bravely into a new future.

CHAPTER ELEVEN

GABE CONTEMPLATED ISLA'S comment about Ellis. She was right. He *did* miss Ellis, but he'd not been thinking of his wife when he'd been dancing with Isla.

Well, not much. He'd briefly thought of her when he'd taken Isla in his arms. A wash of guilt that he'd been holding another woman in his arms. Another woman that he'd wanted to pull close. Wanted to hold. And as they'd danced, as they'd swayed, bodies close, the scent of her dizzying his senses, the feel of her wakening his body so that base, primal desires had been threatening to drown out everything else his brain was capable of thinking about, he had forgotten Ellis. No longer stuck in the past. He had been very much in the present. His breathing ragged. The softness of her fingers in his. The way she'd felt against him. And he'd very much begun to think of the future.

What it would look like for him. For them.

And as thoughts of *them* had filled his brain, of how she might fit into his life, Bea's life, as he'd imagined them together, crazy to believe that he had been doing, Isla's statement had cut through it all.

You must miss Ellis.

Of course he did. But it wasn't as raw as it once had been. The pain of losing Ellis, of realising that he'd been abandoned by her to raise their daughter alone. He'd not told anyone, because he'd felt bad about it, but he'd been angry with Ellis for leaving them, even though he'd known it wasn't her fault. She would not have chosen to die like that. Ellis would have wanted to raise Bea. To be there for her daughter through every step of her life. School. Prom. University. Relationships. Career. Ellis would have wanted to be there for it all. But she wasn't, was she? She never would be. And he'd grown to accept that.

You must miss Ellis.

Why had she said that? Because she meant it? Because she thought that their dancing together was moving too fast? Was it her way of pushing him away? Had she felt his body stirring in response to her? His need, his desire for her, his base thoughts scaring her away because she wasn't ready for anything physical like that? They had kissed. Deep, passionate kisses. Kisses goodnight. Kisses good morning.

He liked kissing her then. He wanted to kiss her more. But the most confusing thing for Gabe was that he was starting to make plans. He could imagine them together so easily. Isla being a part of their life. Isla cooking in the kitchen with him every day. Sharing meals. Cooking with Bea. Going out on trips together. He wanted to take Isla places. Restaurants. Cafes. Theatre. Abroad to different countries and cultures that they could explore together. To India, to share his work with her there. He could imagine them doing that so clearly. So easily.

Bea liked her. No. Scratch that. Bea *loved* Isla. And they'd only spent one weekend together. It was as if they'd been best friends straight away.

He'd not been looking for a mother figure for Bea. He'd not been looking for a relationship at all. But here she was, in their lives, and it was getting complicated.

Isla's statement had simply reminded Gabe that he'd actually *forgotten* his wife. For just a short time. But the cruelty of it was that when he'd been reminded, he'd been holding another woman close, which had somehow made the guilt worse. And he'd felt bad, because it meant, clearly, that he was moving on. Stepping into the next period of his life.

Ellis would have wanted him to be happy, he knew that. She would never have wanted him to be single for the rest of his life, living in solitude to raise his daughter and watch her go out into the world.

'Anything I can do?'

She was putting out two plates. 'You could drain the rice.'

He was glad to be given a job to do. He liked feeling useful. 'Sure.' He placed the colander in the sink and poured the rice into it, draining the water.

Their next patient had come in for a breast reduction. And she'd been very nervous, yet also excited, when Isla had fetched her from the ward for the walk into Theatre. 'I can't believe today is the day. You have no idea how long I've waited for this.'

Isla had smiled. This was what she loved. Knowing that a surgery was about to make a patient's life much better. Laura was petite. Only five feet two. But her breasts were overly large for her frame. 'I bet.'

'Years of backaches. Years of sore indentations in my shoulders from bras that look like they were constructed by the military. Years of wolf whistles and attention I never wanted from men. Being felt up without giving permission. That ends today.'

Now Gabe stood over her, explaining what they were hoping to achieve today.

'Patient would like us to go down to a more comfortable and less painful thirty-four C.'

'She'll have to get used to having a new centre of balance. And she told me that she's really looking forward to buying pretty bras for a change. Little lacy things and attracting guys who like her for who she is rather than the size of her breasts. Do you know she told me that she'd had three guys go out with her who *only* stayed until they'd seen her naked? And then they dropped her.'

'Really? Some guys...' Gabe seemed disgusted as he asked her to pass the scalpel.

Isla had endured wolf whistles from afar before. Stood at a crowded bar and felt someone grab her bottom for a cheap feel. She'd felt the male gaze before, as if they were undressing her with their eyes. And of course there'd been the attack. Where she'd felt that, because she was a woman, she'd been attacked because she was physically weaker than him. That she'd not been seen as a person, as an individual with worth, but just something to be used. How cheap it had made her feel. Her attacker had not been able to force his rage against the loss of his wife, against death, against strokes or infections, and so he'd gone for the easier, more accessible target. As if she were disposable. That was the thought and feeling that had sat in her mind in the first few weeks after the attack. That she was worthless.

It had taken a lot of time for her to find her pride
and her power again. To feel confident.

Gabe didn't make her feel weak. He made her
feel special. As if she was worth something. And
he'd been taking the time to get to know her properly. She loved the way he gazed at her at night,
when they were watching a movie or the television and he thought she hadn't noticed. The way
he'd smile at her. Be considerate of her. Fetch her
drinks. Snacks. Last night? He'd rubbed her feet
for her. That had been…interesting.

They'd been watching some action flick. One
of her favourite actors. Isla had been at one end
of the couch, Gabe the other. Her legs had been
aching that day. She'd done a lot of steps at work
and so she'd lifted her feet up onto the couch and
Gabe had just lifted them onto his lap and begun
massaging them!

It had been heavenly! His fingers expertly massaging out the knots and aches in her arches, her
soles, her toes. His warm hands smoothing over
her skin, over tired muscles in her lower legs, ma-
nipulating her ankles, his thumbs applying soft
pressure, his fingers stroking her.

It had taken every ounce of willpower for her to
not moan with pleasure. And when the film was
over? She'd closed her eyes and sunk further into
the cushions and allowed him to continue. To feel
him touching her, in a non-sexual way, but giv-

ing her pleasure, was almost orgasmic. To realise that she could be touched by a man and not feel threatened. To realise that she could trust Gabe to respect her boundaries. He hadn't tried to run his hand further up her legs. He hadn't tried to pull her closer to touch her elsewhere. He hadn't tried to make it sexual.

Yet somehow, it had been. To her, anyway.

And the most wonderful thing about it? She had, briefly, wanted him to. She'd thought, *What would it feel like to have him trail his fingers up my calf, past my knee and up my thigh?* The thought had made her heart pound, had made her groin ache and her breathing increase, but at the same time, she'd been terrified. So much so, she'd opened her eyes, smiled at him and reluctantly pulled her feet free of his manipulations.

'Thank you,' she'd said.

'You're welcome.'

He'd smiled back at her and his eyes had been so dark and mysterious, she'd wondered what he'd been thinking, too. Had he been holding back? Had he wanted to do the same thing to her? Allow his hands to go exploring? Wandering? When she'd gone to bed that night, she'd lain there, clutching at her duvet, thinking about Gabe lying in his own bed just a few doors away.

Had he been thinking of her, the way she'd been thinking of him?

Gabe carefully made an incision around the nipple, the areola and down each midline of the breast. 'Tell me, what are the risks of breast reduction?'

She liked it when he quizzed her.

'Bruising. Numbness. Sometimes there can be a difficulty with breastfeeding afterwards. Sometimes the nipples don't take and they can be lost. But that's rare.'

He nodded. 'And why am I using liposuction?'

'To remove excess fatty tissue in each breast. It helps to reduce the volume.'

'Good.'

Liposuction always looked quite violent, but the results from it could be very good indeed. It did create a soreness and tenderness after the surgery, but that could be managed with pain medication and maintaining movement in those areas, so that the patient didn't stiffen up.

'I'm now going to reshape the breasts to try and maintain what?'

'Similarity in size and shape, but the breasts may be different after surgery once swelling has gone down.'

'Good. You know your stuff.'

'I've watched you do this twice before and your results have been terrific. Seeing the ladies come in for check-ups afterwards? They seem so happy with their surgery.'

'That's what it's all about. I'm going to place the drains now.' He sewed the drains into position. One under each breast so that any extra blood or fluid might drain away into two holding pots at the end of each drain. The Garland Clinic offered patients special bags that the drains could be held in, so the patient didn't have to carry them around.

'It's looking good,' she said. 'She's going to be happy, I think.'

'Okay. Are you happy to do the bandages and the support bra?'

'Absolutely!'

'All right. I'm done! Let's get her to Recovery and monitor her, but she should be able to go home by the end of the day.'

'Perfect.'

At the rear of the Garland Clinic, there was a small walled, private garden with a bench, beneath a pergola. If the weather was nice, sometimes the staff would sit out there and eat their lunch, or, if they were on a morning or afternoon break, sit out there with a coffee or tea.

Today was one of those days. The weather was surprisingly warm. There was almost no breeze and the sun was shining brightly. They'd just finished Laura's surgery and it had gone well. Isla had escorted Laura up to Recovery and she was under observation for a few hours, before she'd be allowed home.

Isla had been thinking about what Gabe had said. About changing people's lives and how easily they could manage that with a few cuts and a few well-placed sutures. Of course, there was more to it than that, but, at the end of the day, that was what it was.

Isla wished she could remove the memory of her attack. Her life would be so much easier if that particular scar on her soul could be excised. Was it possible? Would she ever be able to forget?

'You look lost in thought.' Gabe's voice came from behind her and she turned on the bench to see him coming towards her, with two mugs. 'Brought you a tea.'

'Thanks.' She took the tea from him.

'Penny for them?'

'Just thinking about the past, that's all.'

'Oh. Past good, or past bad?'

'Past bad. Wondering how to excise the stuff you don't want. Make the new you happier with yourself. More confident.'

She knew he'd understand. He dealt with people who tried to do that every day. 'Well, you have three options. Option one, you accept who you are, warts and all. Accept that you are unique and that it's not the cards that you're dealt, but how you play them.'

She smiled. 'I'm not sure I want to play these cards.'

'Okay, option two is…you find a way to move forward. Get rid of what you don't need. Refuse to let baggage hold you back. Go forth no matter what and let the past be damned.'

'And option three?'

'You find someone to help you. Someone who makes you feel better about option one.' He smiled at her. 'That's what I did.'

Isla raised an eyebrow. 'Who? Ellis?'

'No. It was you.'

'Me?'

'My life was just fine before you came along. At least I thought so. But then you arrived and something changed. My life is brighter. Happier. I feel more content. I'm looking forward to my daughter coming home tonight.' He joked, winking at her, before taking a sip of his tea.

Isla laughed. 'So what you're saying is that my life could be heaps better with the right person by my side.'

'Yes.' He raised his mug as if toasting the suggestion.

She clinked it with hers. 'And how do I know who that person is?'

'I think you'll know instantly. Deep down in your heart. It may be hidden to begin with. Covered over by thick blankets of fear, or shame or denial. But you'll know, because that person will be the one you think of all the time. The person that is never out of your thoughts. The person who you imagine doing things with, even if that scares you.'

'You're all of those things,' she said quickly, not having realised that she wanted to say it, but it had just come out anyway. As if she'd wanted to say it, before she got too scared to if she thought about it first. She felt her cheeks colour at having showed her cards. Her thoughts. Her feelings.

He smiled and looked her directly in the eye. 'You're all of those things for me, too.' He looked back at the clinic, made sure that they couldn't be seen from the door, or windows, and then he leaned over and planted a kiss on her lips.

She felt a thrill run through her at his words. He felt the same way? She'd hoped, but he'd not actually said anything and so she hadn't wanted to assume.

But his words made her happy.

'You've changed my life,' he said softly when the kiss ended, looking deeply into her eyes.

Isla stared back at him. Shocked. Surprised. Happy. Afraid. They'd known each other mere weeks and yet they'd become so close, so quickly, from having spent so much time together. If they meant this much to each other already, what did that mean? Where was this thing going? Because if it was going to get serious, Gabe might expect more from her. Physically.

And what if she couldn't?

What if the past stopped her?

Because she didn't want to lose someone as incredible as him.

'You've changed mine too,' she said, reaching up to stroke his face, wishing she could tell him so much more. Admit to so much more. But she was afraid her words might entrap her further. Maybe it would be best to hold back until she was sure of whether she could be physical? Maybe they should put on the brakes? She'd thought about going home. About getting some space from him. But then she'd promised to stay until after her birthday on Sunday. To still be there for when Bea came home, so they could spend her birthday weekend together.

And that was another thing. If she got involved with Gabe seriously, then she would become a stepmother of sorts to Beatrice. Was she ready for that? Prepared for all that that would mean?

'I should go back in,' she whispered and kissed him quickly one more time, before getting up and leaving him alone on the bench. She hated walking away. She hated leaving him. She'd wanted him to say more. To tell her all the things she wanted to hear.

But she'd been scared. Because if he'd said all those lovely things, the three words she longed to hear, she would have been terrified of saying them too.

CHAPTER TWELVE

THIS TIME WHEN she volunteered to go with him to collect Bea from school, he agreed. There was nothing more he wanted than to spend as much time as possible with Isla. Because he had no idea if she would even be with him after her birthday weekend and so he wanted to enjoy every second. She had become incredibly important to him and, this weekend, he planned to sit with Bea and ask her how she truly felt about their house guest. Because it was one thing to get along with someone if you thought of them as just a guest, or a friend, but quite another to consider having that person in your life more permanently, as a mother figure.

So, the more time he gave them to bond, the better.

As usual, the traffic was heavy. Maybe even heavier than it had been last week. They were stuck in bumper-to-bumper traffic at a point that didn't usually get congested and he was having a difficult time trying to see past the cars in front of him, to find out why. But as they inched forward, they both became aware of flashing lights. Car hazard lights and, beyond that, debris on the road. Long scaffolding poles and broken glass. An accident? There were no emergency service vehicles there yet, so it must have just happened.

'We ought to stop. See if we need to provide assistance,' Isla said, taking the words right out of his mouth.

As he parked up, off to one side, he put on his own hazards and Isla rushed off to give assistance as he removed the orange cones he kept in the back of his vehicle in case of breakdown. It was one thing to offer help, but you needed to be safe to do so. They were out and vulnerable on a busy roadside. Then he ran to catch up. He had a basic first-aid kit in his car, but it was only gauze pads, bandages, plasters, gloves. He grabbed the gloves and passed them to Isla as they assessed the driver and passenger in the car.

A scaffolding pole must have fallen from the lorry far up ahead, bounced onto the road and then up and through the windscreen. The driver must have swerved and hit the metal barrier on the side of the road. Luckily, the pole had gone through the centre point, missing both driver and passenger, but they had multiple cuts from broken glass, were both in shock and the passenger's legs were crushed into a tiny space where the side of their car had crumpled in. Unfortunately, they'd been driving a classic car and so it didn't have the safety reinforced cage that modern cars had.

Gabe glanced ahead. The driver of the truck with the scaffolding poles was getting out of his cab and beginning to run back to offer assistance. He was fine. There were no pedestrians or other vehicles involved, so they could focus on these two people. He pulled his mobile from his pocket and dialled 999, informing them of the situation.

'Emergency services are en route to your position, sir.'

'Inform them that there is a doctor and nurse on scene.'

The female passenger was crying, hiccupping breaths. The male driver was calmer.

'Sir, tell me your name.'

'Paul. And this is my wife, Janelle.'

They were an older couple. Maybe mid-seventies? 'Any medical history I should know about, Paul?'

'I'm on blood thinners.'

That would explain the profuse bleeding he was having from his head.

'My wife has high blood pressure and is being treated for lung cancer. We've just come back from the hospital. She's had chemo today.'

Gabe's heart sank. That wasn't good. 'Okay, Paul, Janelle. I'm Gabe and I'm a doctor and the fine young lady next to your wife is Isla and she's

a nurse. We're going to help you until the paramedics get here. What I'm going to do is ask you
both to sit very still, whilst I perform a primary
survey on you both, okay?'

It had been a long time since Gabe had worked
in Accident and Emergency. He'd done a few
months' worth of shifts there as a junior doctor
and, though he'd enjoyed it, he'd not enjoyed the
tragedies. The upsetting stories where he felt as
though, no matter what they did, they could not
save a life. Or change a life. Or make someone
better. He'd lost count of how many times he'd
taken a patient's family members into a family
room to break bad news and it had almost broken him. He'd got out of A & E as quickly as he
could. Not entirely sure where he wanted to specialise in those early, exhausting years.

Behind him, cars crept by. He was aware of
stares, of being watched. Even of people with
their phones out, recording as he assessed Paul
and Janelle. Paul was in pretty decent shape considering what had happened. Shock, cuts and
abrasions, and undoubtedly whiplash, but without
scans and X-rays he couldn't be sure of anything.
He would need to maintain Paul's cervical spine,
so he told Paul to sit still and not move, whilst
he assessed Paul's wife. She was in much worse
shape, losing consciousness, and her entrapped
legs looked as though they might be broken be-

neath the knee. Isla maintained Janell's C-spine as Gabe clambered into the back to hold Paul's head steady.

He could hear sirens now. Could feel relief flooding through him at their approach. Even Paul reached out to grab his wife's hand and squeeze it reassuringly. 'They're nearly here, Paul. Janelle will get the help she needs and pain relief to make her more comfortable.' Thankfully, Janelle was still breathing evenly as she drifted in and out of consciousness.

Gabe glanced at Isla, who knelt beside him in the back seat of Paul and Janelle's car. Her eyes were full of fear. 'It'll be okay,' he whispered as paramedics arrived in view and asked Gabe for an update on the situation.

He told them what he could. They placed cervical collars on Paul and then Janelle. Paul was taken out of his vehicle relatively easily and placed into an ambulance and taken away, though it took longer for Janelle. Police took their statements and they were told that they could go. They needed to. Gabe was very much aware that Beatrice would be wondering where they were.

'Honey? It's Dad. Sorry we're running late, but there was an accident. We weren't involved, we're fine, but we had to stop to render assistance,' he said, calling her on his mobile before he started driving again.

'Oh, okay. I guess I'll see you soon, then?'

'Half an hour. Tops.' He couldn't wait to hold his daughter safely in his arms. It was at moments like this, when life came close to death, that people felt the need to hug their loved ones close. When Gabe had lost Ellis and he'd been all alone in the hospital, except for his poorly newborn baby daughter, he had held her in his arms and gazed into her little face and wondered what her life would be like without a mother. He'd not been sure he'd be up to the task of parenting alone. He'd been scared and then her oxygen alarms had gone off and nurses had rushed in and taken Beatrice from him and put tubes down her and he'd stood there, shocked, listening to the alarms on her machines, and backed away, not sure if he had the strength to lose her too.

But something had kept him there. Hope. Fear. Those two opposing forces had bound him to stay. He had been the one left. The one responsible for her. She'd no longer had a mother, she'd needed a father to fight for her and he'd vowed to do that every day of her life. Determined to bring her up right, and maybe he'd gone about that the wrong way, which was why they'd begun to feel a separation between them, but Isla was the glue putting them back together. He reached across for Isla's hand, as Paul had done to Janelle, and squeezed her fingers.

'You okay?' she asked.

'Yeah. You?'

'I think so. That was scary, huh?'

'Yeah. But I'm no stranger to scary.'

She nodded. 'Nor me.'

'Doesn't mean we're experts, though, does it? We still stumble blindly through the difficult parts of life.'

Isla laughed. 'Ain't that the truth? Do you think we'll ever be experts? Do you think we'll ever be confronted with something scary and just brush it off and calmly wade through it, anyway?'

'I'd like to think so. But maybe scary is there for a reason? Maybe being scared is what propels us to be better? To have faith in ourselves. Or more confidence. Maybe we should view scary as an opportunity for personal growth?'

'Gabriel Newton, plastic surgeon extraordinaire *and* philosopher.'

He smiled. 'You know what I mean.'

'I do. In fact I've been thinking about fear a lot just lately.'

'You have?'

'Of course. This situation we're in…that's scary. My feelings for you…*us*…that's scary.'

He made the turning into Hardwicke then. He wanted to answer her, to say something wise and important and considered, but he couldn't think of what to say, so he said nothing as he drove up the long driveway to the front door, where Beatrice was waiting with her tutor, Mr Sansom.

Bea gave him a lovely hug when he got out of the car and then she hugged Isla, too.

He couldn't help but smile.

'Mr Newton? Might I have a word?' asked Mr Sansom.

Gabe looked at Isla.

'Bea? Let's get your bags in the car, whilst your dad talks.'

He was grateful for Isla to distract his daughter. 'What's up?' he asked.

'I just wanted to make you aware that Beatrice has had to make one or two visits to the school nurse this week, due to her coughing. She seems fine, but I can't help but worry that maybe her cystic fibrosis is taking a turn and I thought it best to keep you updated. I did email you during the week about it. I assume you saw that?'

Gabe frowned. There had been an email from school, but he'd not read it. Normally when he got emails from the school, it was about events or fundraising, or concerts, never anything important like this. He felt bad for not reading it. 'You should have tried to call me.'

'I did, but you were unavailable at the time. In surgery, I do believe, so I left a message with your secretary.'

Damn. It must be somewhere in my inbox and I never saw it!

'Right. Well, thank you for letting me know. I'll do an assessment at home and keep an eye on her.'

'Of course. You have a good weekend, Mr Newton.'

'You too.'

Gabe clambered into the car, feeling a niggly worry at the back of his mind. Was Bea's CF getting worse, or had she just had a rough week? Her coughing had been worse after the concert. Had she picked up an infection? Or was this nothing? Was this Bea's tutor being overly cautious?

'Ready to get home?' he asked, looking into the back seat.

As if on cue, Bea coughed heavily, then nodded, her eyes watering.

He felt something strange and dangerous settle in his stomach and, with a feeling of foreboding, he drove home.

CHAPTER THIRTEEN

'I WANT TO take you into work. Show you around,' Gabe said to Bea when she'd finished her morning clearance exercises.

'Really?'

'Yes. I'd like to show you where I work. What I do.' He looked a bit twitchy.

'And…?' Bea asked, raising an eyebrow.

'And we have machines and equipment there so I can check you out a bit.'

'There we go.' Bea looked smug. 'That's what Mr Sansom was talking to you about, huh? That my cough had been bad last week?'

Gabe smiled. Caught out. 'He may have mentioned it briefly. Don't you want to see where I work?'

'I do. I'm kind of interested in medicine, actually. But you don't need to worry about me, Dad. I'm fine. We'd been trampolining and I may have just done more of it than I should.'

'Trampolining?' Gabe sounded concerned. 'Bea, you know you have to be careful.'

'I know, Dad, but you've got to trust me.'

Gabe had been so worried last night, he'd sat on the stairs, listening to Bea cough in her bedroom. Her tutor's comment had really unnerved him and he'd even considered getting her old baby monitor out of storage and putting it in her room.

I'm not sure Bea would like the idea of you monitoring her with video and audio now that she's nearly a teenager in her own room,' Isla had said.

'I can hear you guys! If you're gonna chat out there, can you do it quieter? Some of us are trying to sleep!'

They'd both smiled and headed downstairs, but they'd stayed up later than normal, enjoying a glass of wine, and right before they'd gone to bed, Isla had even massaged Gabe's shoulders. He'd felt so tense! But she'd soon soothed out his knots and to hear him sigh with pleasure had made her feel good, too.

When they arrived at the Garland Clinic, that Saturday morning, it felt strange to be there. Of course, it was empty of patients, but Phillip Garland was there, in his office, catching up on some paperwork, and the cleaners were in, working hard.

Gabe introduced Bea to his boss and then showed her his own consulting room.

Bea looked around it, smiling. 'This is all yours?'

'Yes.'

'You have a picture of Mum and me on your desk.' Bea picked up the framed photo and smiled at it.

'Yes.'

Isla wanted to slip her hand into his. To comfort him. This was a big thing for the two of them. They were reconnecting in ways that Gabe could never have imagined just a few short weeks ago.

Bea put the picture down. 'Where do you operate?'

'Theatre. I'll take you, but you mustn't touch anything.'

'Really? You don't want me touching sharp scalpels and things? Shocking.' She laughed and followed him down the corridor towards the theatres.

Isla followed them, watching them walk side by side as Gabe gave his daughter the tour. They entered Theatre and Bea marvelled at the bright lights, the equipment and the 'cutting table', as she called it.

'Does this ever drip with blood? Like, do you have to mop it up off the floor?' she asked with marvellous glee.

'Thankfully, no.' Gabe smiled.

At that moment, Isla's phone rang. 'Excuse me for a minute.' And she went to take her call.

* * *

When Isla was gone, he took a chest X-ray of Bea to make sure her lungs looked okay, before he asked her the question that had been on his mind for a while. 'Can I ask…what do you think of Isla?'

Bea turned to look him right in the eye. 'She's great. I really like her. She's made you a happier person.'

He smiled. 'You think so?'

'Think so? I know so! I've never seen you smile so much. Weekends are a little less stressful now.'

'You noticed that?'

'I notice a lot of things, Dad. You like her, huh?'

He sucked in a breath. 'I do. I like her a lot. She's been hurt before and I don't want to make any mistakes in causing her any more pain.'

'Sure.'

'And so I wanted to check in with you, now that we can talk to one another, about how you'd feel about Isla becoming…' He didn't know how to finish off the sentence.

'Becoming your girlfriend?' Bea smiled, finishing it for him.

He guessed girlfriend was as good a term as any for now. 'Yeah.'

And he would absolutely go by Bea's decision. It was important. He wanted to show Bea that he respected her too. She was growing up now, as

Isla had said. He had to respect her as a growing woman. She was becoming her own person. Independent. Which was what he'd wanted when he'd sent her to Hardwicke. She was strong. Wilful. In many ways she was just like her mother. And he would not enter any serious relationship without his daughter's approval of any woman that would become a serious component of her life.

'I think she's great. You should go for it.'

'Really?'

Bea nodded. 'Really.'

He gave Bea a hug then. Really squeezed her tight, laid his head on top of hers. They were still hugging when Isla came back into the room, her face grim.

'What's wrong?' he asked, feeling a deep concern rise up at the look on her face.

'There's an article about us. It's everywhere.'

Back home, Gabe turned his monitor so that she could see and there, emblazoned across the screen, were pictures of her and Gabe at the road traffic accident, obviously taken by a passer-by in a car, and her whole identity revealed.

Gabe's mystery blonde turns heroine at roadside!

It was all there in black and white. The accident yesterday, her and Gabe helping out, but it seemed that someone had managed to talk to Paul and Janelle, who'd wanted to thank the couple that had helped them roadside and named them. From that, it had taken whichever gutter journalist this was to discover her past and share it in the article.

She felt herself grow cold.

It was out. Everyone would know now.

'I don't believe it. How did they find out?'

'How do they find anything out? They dig and dig until they strike gold. I'm so sorry, Isla. I tried to protect you as much as I could.'

She nodded, but already her mind was racing with thoughts. Feelings. But overall, she felt kind of resigned to it. 'Maybe it's a good thing that it's out now.'

Gabe looked up at her, confused. 'How do you mean?'

'Well…hiding a part of my past, pretending that everything is fine, trying to be someone new, wearing a mask…it's *exhausting*, Gabe! Maybe now I can just be me and if people want to talk about it, let them. Because look at what it's done to me so far. I changed my name, I lost my marriage, my job that I loved. I moved away, got a new job and had to move into your house, uprooting *your* personal life, just to protect mine!'

'I didn't mind. I've loved having you here. So has Bea.'

'I know.' She smiled at him. 'But there's no

point in hiding any more. They all know. The world and his wife. I should just go back to my friend's flat and start again.'

'After your birthday? As promised?'

Another smile. He was being so sweet. So nice. To show that he wasn't eager to get rid of her, and she appreciated that. 'After my birthday.'

'I think I'm getting a cold.' Bea stood in the doorway to the kitchen and she did indeed look a little poorly. Her nose was red, she was sniffing and wiping her nose with a tissue and as soon as she finished, she sneezed, which set off a coughing fit.

Gabe walked her over to the table and sat her down. 'Your chest X-ray was good though. I'll get you some decongestants. Isla, could you do her a hot water with honey and lemon?'

'Sure.'

He sat down with his daughter at the table and reached for her hand. 'Anything I can do?'

'Let me eat ice cream?'

'No.'

She smiled. 'Worth a shot.'

Gabe grinned. He liked this easy nature they had between them now. Now that they could talk to one another without it always being a battle of wills. Why couldn't he have seen what his daughter needed before now? He'd believed that, being

Bea's only parent, he had to be really hard on discipline to make sure that she grew up with the right head on her shoulders, but he'd forgotten all the rest that she'd needed. A soft place to fall. Someone who would listen. Someone who would let the occasional thing slide and who would take an interest in her likes and needs. He'd been so focused on staying on top of her CF, not exposing her to risk, that he'd never thought about music concerts or taking a step back from the role of disciplinarian.

Isla had taught him differently. In one short weekend, she'd shown him what was possible and he knew now to not have a knee-jerk reaction where his daughter was concerned.

'Here. Sip this. But be careful. It's hot,' Isla said, setting down a mug and pressing the backs of her fingers to Bea's head. 'No temperature, so that's good.'

'We need you to be better for tomorrow.'

'Isla's birthday? What are we doing?'

'I thought a show at the West End and then dinner for all three of us, but if you're ill, then maybe we should postpone?'

'It's just a cold! I'll be fine. Which show are we seeing?' she asked.

'You can help me decide.' Isla smiled.

Isla woke to the sound of two people badly singing 'Happy Birthday' as her bedroom door was

opened and in walked Gabe and Bea, with a birthday cake with a fizzing sparkler candle on it.
Laughing, she sat up in bed and waited for Gabe
to deposit the cake on her lap. As the candle fiz-
zled out, she clapped her hands. 'Thanks, guys!
Is this why you wanted me to have a lie-in?'

'Yes. We get to spoil *you* today.'

'Aww, you don't have to do that. How are you
feeling, Bea?' Yesterday, Bea had coughed and
sneezed her way through the day, and they'd ended
up vegging on the couch and watching movies
and, eventually, Bea had got her ice cream.

'I'm fine. Just the sniffles and sneezes.'

'How were your clearance exercises this morning?' She'd heard her going through her routine
downstairs.

'Same as always. No better, no worse. Dad can
stop panicking.'

Isla looked to Gabe for confirmation and he
gave a nod as he passed her two birthday cards.
'Happy birthday, from both of us.'

Isla thanked them and began to open their
cards. The one from Bea had a dazed, scruffy-
looking dog on the front, with hair sticking in all
directions. It said, *You don't look that old!* and
inside was a message that read, *Happy Birthday,
Isla! Hope you have a lovely day! Love Bea.* With
three kisses.

'Thanks, Bea.'

Gabe's card had a teddy bear on the front, and the teddy was holding a big bunch of beautiful flowers. Inside, the message read, *Happy Birthday, Isla. You're the gift in my life. Love Gabe.* With a single kiss.

'Thank you.' She wanted to kiss him, but Bea was there and they'd not really spoken to Bea about the two of them having feelings for one another. Or so she'd thought.

Because in that moment, Gabe stooped to drop a kiss on her cheek.

She blushed and glanced at Bea, but Bea was smiling.

'It's cool. I know. By the way, I made you this.' Bea passed over a small wrapped present, tied with a pink bow.

She knew? When had Gabe talked to her? 'You made me something? Bea!' She reached forward to give Bea a hug, then tore into the wrapping and discovered a small purse that had a hand-embroidered flower on it.

'I made it in textile class.'

Her heart was overflowing. 'Bea, it's beautiful. I'll treasure it always.'

Bea beamed. 'What do you want for breakfast?'

'You're making it?'

'I am.'

Isla glanced at Gabe, who gave her a small nod to let her know that Bea would not be left unsupervised in the kitchen and that he'd be helping. Gabe had been getting better in the kitchen, but what would be the easiest thing for them to prepare? 'Poached egg on toast?'

'Coming right up.' Gabe leaned in and this time dropped a kiss upon her lips, before he stood and removed the cake.

Isla flushed, glancing at Bea to see her reaction, but Bea was just smiling at the two of them and when her dad had begun going downstairs, Bea turned in the doorway and said, 'He likes you a lot, you know. He said you'd been hurt before, but…please don't hurt him. He's been through enough.'

Isla stared at Bea. 'I like him a lot. He's a very kind, generous man.'

Bea smiled and headed downstairs to help cook breakfast.

He felt an element of nervousness as he got dressed for going out with Bea and Isla. Gabe might have been seen out with some of the most known female celebrities out there, but he had never been seen out and about with another woman *and* his daughter at the same time. He knew what the press would make of it and he'd warned Isla, too, but she'd simply sucked in a deep breath and said, *'Fine.'*

He was proud of her for not being scared of

them any more. She was most definitely stronger than him. To him, the press had become something he had acquired. A thorn in his side. Something that had become a nuisance. Honestly, sometimes he'd been photographed just going out to get milk. But Isla? She wasn't going to let them see that she was bothered any more. They'd found out her biggest secret, they'd written about her past and splurged it across their pages and, quite frankly? Isla was of the opinion of what else could they do to her? Nothing, was the answer. They might speculate, they might ask her for a quote, they might chase her with their cameras, but she was refusing to run any more and for that he admired her.

It took strength to do that. And he'd discovered, since getting to know Isla, just how strong that she was.

He couldn't believe that she would leave after today! He didn't want that. He really wanted her to stay. He loved having her here. Loved waking up in the morning to the sounds of her in his kitchen. Sometimes she'd hum to music, or be singing in that cute, off-key way that she had.

He loved sitting across from her at the breakfast table and discussing their upcoming patients for that day. He loved the drive in to work with her. They'd listen to the radio and there'd be a music quiz on that one station they listened to and they'd both try to outdo the other. On the drive home, they'd let off steam, and at home, they'd cook together and then eat together and watch a movie or series that was streaming.

He loved the way she smelt when she came downstairs after a bath or shower, her hair wrapped up in a towel on top of her head. He loved the way she felt snuggled next to him on the couch. He loved the way they'd kiss each other goodnight. He loved knowing that she was sleeping, safe and secure, just a few rooms away from his at night. And he loved that Bea loved her too.

After today? All of that would be gone.

He'd be living alone again all week. Seeing her only at work, and he knew it would not be enough.

Somehow, he would like to convince her to stay. But how? What if she thought it was moving too fast?

I'll start by giving her a birthday to remember.

Once he was in his tux, he went to check that Bea was ready, only to discover Bea was being helped to choose her outfit by Isla, who looking stunning in an emerald wraparound dress and heels.

He'd seen her once in heels before. At the new employee dinner. They emphasised her shapely calves and the swish of her skirt as she moved. Her waist was neat and gently rounded, perfecting her hourglass figure. And she'd done something remarkable with her hair, curling her normally straight blonde hair so that it fell in gentle waves around her neck and shoulders. Her eyes smouldered and her lips, highlighted by a lipstick, looked edible.

'Wow! You look amazing!' he managed to say.

Isla smiled at him, her eyes looking him up and down. 'So do you. Now all we have to do is find a dress for Bea. We can't decide between the red or the blue.' She held up two dresses on their hangers. 'She likes the red one, but feels the blue might be more appropriate for a restaurant. What do you think?'

Gabe glanced at his daughter, feeling as though this question was some sort of test for him to pass and he wanted to get it right. So he thought for a moment. 'The blue might be more appropriate for the restaurant, but, if I remember correctly, the last time you wore it, you said the elastic at the waist irritated your skin, so I'm going to say the red one, because I know you have the perfect shoes to match.' He waited with bated breath to see if she would approve.

Bea grinned and nodded at Isla.

He'd passed!

'Red, it is. We'll leave you to get dressed. Call me if you need me to do the zip at the back.' Isla left the room with him, closing the door softly behind her. 'Well done.'

'Thank you,' he said, feeling kind of smug.

'You know there was a secret third option?' Isla asked him with a tilted head and a smile.

'Ah, you mean the white dress with the butterflies on it?'

'I do!'

'But she won't wear that at night, because bright lights shine through it, so I discarded it as an option.'

'You have been taking notes!'

'All thanks to you.' He leaned forward and dropped a soft kiss upon her lips. He'd been wanting to do that all day. The desire to touch her and hold her had been getting stronger of late. He wanted to do so many things to her. To explore her. Taste her. But he'd been holding back. Holding back even more with Bea here. 'You know I had the chance to speak to Bea briefly when I gave her the work tour.'

'I do.'

'About you. Us. What her thoughts were on there possibly being an us.'

Isla stopped smiling and looked serious. 'And what did she say?'

'She said she didn't mind. That she liked you a lot and could see that you made me happy.'

She seemed to relax again. 'Oh. Good! I'm glad.'

'Me too.' He reached for her fingers with his.

Felt them entwine. Imagined their bodies entwining and brushed his lips over her neck, inhaling her scent, only to break away guiltily when Bea's door suddenly opened and his daughter came out and asked Isla to do her zip.

He glanced at his watch as a distraction exercise. 'We ought to start making a move or we'll miss curtain up.'

'Okay. Let's go!'

CHAPTER FOURTEEN

ISLA HAD NEVER been to the theatre before to see a
show. She'd been to the cinema, but never a show,
or even a music concert, except for the one with
Bea. And they had to go to a matinee showing
and then eat around six, to get Bea back to Hardwicke by late evening. So the show was a treat.
A special experience in which she loved everything about it. She'd not been sure how engrossed
she would be in the story, but there were music,
songs, laughter and even a moment where she
found herself leaning forward, so caught up in the
moment that she actually found tears in her eyes
at the end, when the lead female character might
lose everything she had fought for. When the cast
came on stage to take their bows and applause,
she stood and clapped the loudest. If she knew
how to wolf-whistle? She'd have done that, too.

'That was amazing!' she said to Gabe as they
came out of the theatre and headed to the car so
that they could drive to their dinner reservation.

'Wasn't it?'

'I really liked the prince,' said Bea. 'He was funny.'

Isla turned to look at her and smiled. 'He was so funny!' She laughed, thinking of his antics. 'How's your cold?'

'I'm all right. Just a blocked nose, mostly.'

'And how does your chest feel? No tightness?'

'No.' And, as if prompted, she coughed to show that she could without it overwhelming her. 'Where are we going to eat?'

'De Luca's. It's Italian,' said Gabe.

'Yes! I see a pizza in my future!' said Bea, rubbing her hands together.

Isla smiled and turned back to Gabe. He looked happy. Content. She wanted to reach out and lay her hand on his, but she was nervous with Bea there, watching, even though she now knew that Bea wasn't opposed to them being together. Dared she?

'Have we been there before?'

'No. But I picked it because it has good reviews and there's a kids' area there, where you can play video games if you get bored of being with grown-ups.'

'Cool!'

Isla smiled. If Bea did go off to play on the video games, perhaps she and Gabe could share a nice moment together? That would be wonderful, as the time before she had to return home was ticking by so quickly. Now she'd made the decision to leave, she was beginning to regret it.

What was waiting for her back at her friend's flat? Damp. That window that, even when closed, still produced a draft. Empty rooms. Stuff that didn't even belong to her, but to her friend. All that was hers were her suitcase and some food in the fridge that had probably gone off by now, anyway, so...

But there was no reason to stay here any more. Her secret was out and the whole reason for her staying with Gabe had been to protect that secret. There was nothing to protect any more and so she had to go. She couldn't expect Gabe and Bea to keep putting up with her. Those two needed their space to grow and it would be good for Isla and Gabe to get some space. Living in each other's pockets was fine at the start of a relationship when they were still in a honeymoon period and everything was fresh and new and exciting, but if this relationship was to move at a steady pace, then they'd each need their own space to breathe. Because sometimes, being with Gabe, she felt that she couldn't think clearly. Especially when his lips were at her neck and her hands were in his, or when kisses grew more passionate and her senses assailed her.

Isla smiled as they entered De Luca's. It was deceptively intimate. Lots of round tables. Candlelight. Soft piano music. White table linens and a single rose in a bud vase on each table. Wooden panelling adorned with awards for cooking and pictures of various celebrities with the chef blocked off the view of an area filled with computers and consoles, but a small screen in the corner allowed them to keep an eye on Bea as she went to explore it.

The waiter came and took their order. Gabe ordered a plain cheese pizza for Bea as she'd requested, with doughballs and a salad, and Isla and Gabe ordered arancini for starters and *branzino* for main—oven-baked sea bass, with lemon, garlic, herbs and a white-wine fennel sauce.

As the pianist tickled the ivories, Isla sat forward to look Gabe in the eyes. 'Thank you for this. I'm loving every moment of my birthday with you and Bea.'

He sat forward too. Reached for her hand. 'I'm glad. I wanted to spoil you and I am, though if we'd had to spend your birthday, at home, in jammies, watching a movie on the couch, I would have tried to make that special, too.'

'Any time with you is special,' she said, smiling. Meaning it. Meeting Gabe had changed her life. He'd gone from being her boss to someone close. Someone she truly adored. She knew she could trust him and that meant a huge deal, because she'd not thought she'd ever learn to trust a man again.

It gave her hope. That, one day, she might attain all those things she'd ever dreamed of. A marriage. A family. She'd once thought—feared— that she would always be alone, but maybe now that wouldn't be the case?

When the food arrived, they called Bea back to the table and they sat and ate together as a family. It felt nice. Isla was happy. Bea and Gabe were great company. Funny, warm, companionable. They all laughed at the same things and she could feel herself get excited for things that Bea had coming up at school. She was going to audition for the school's end-of-year production and they talked about what her audition piece could be and Isla really hoped that Bea would do well.

Gabe chatted a little about his next trip to India, telling her all about the work he did out there. 'And I'd love it if you'd come with me, Isla.'

India! 'I've never been. I've never been out of Europe. In fact, the farthest I've ever been is France. Are you *sure*, Gabe?'

'Absolutely. I think you'd make a vital contribution to the work over there. We always need good surgical nurses and I think it would be a brilliant experience for you.' He paused. 'And I'd like you there with me.' He reached for her hand. Squeezed it.

It was a big decision. One that excited her. 'Well, yes. I'd love to! Thank you!' she gushed.

He leaned in, pecked her on the cheek and she coloured.

As expected, when they came out of the restaurant, she found herself looking for photographers, but there weren't any, thankfully.

On the drive home to get changed and collect Bea's things for school, Bea was yawning heavily and coughing a lot. She needed to do her evening clearance exercises before returning to Hardwicke and so they were doing their level best to keep her entertained. But once they were home, they had an hour or two before they needed to get going and Isla popped upstairs to get changed out of her dress and into something more comfortable for taking Bea back to Hardwicke.

It was going to be hard to say goodbye to Bea, because, after today, she wasn't sure when she'd next get to see her. Hopefully next weekend, if she and Gabe arranged something.

She removed the dress and placed it on a hanger and wrapped herself in a bathrobe whilst she decided what to wear, and was standing in front of her wardrobe, lost in her thoughts, when she heard a gentle knock on her bedroom door.

'Come in,' she said, expecting Bea.

But it was Gabe.

She smiled at him and self-consciously pulled

her bathrobe more tightly closed. 'Hey. Thank you for today. I had a great time.'

'Me too.'

He closed her bedroom door behind him and came to stand beside her. 'I can't believe you won't be here tomorrow. My life won't be the same.'

She smiled. 'Nor mine.' She leant into the wardrobe, grabbed a pair of jeans and a light blue sweater, only for Gabe to turn her towards him. Pull her close and look deeply into her eyes.

'Would it be wrong of me to say I don't want you to go?' He looked truly conflicted.

'Of course not. It shows you care about me.'

'I do. I truly do. And I never thought I'd feel this way about someone else. I'm beginning to believe that everything just might turn out great. That I won't lose everyone I love.'

Love. Was he saying he loved her?

Isla leant in. Kissed him. 'I feel the same way, too.'

He seemed to think for a moment. 'Then don't. Don't go. Stay with me.'

She hesitated. Actually thought about it. 'But what would that mean?'

'Whatever you want it to mean.'

'Like a real relationship? Something we'd admit to everyone? All the people we work with? Our families? Friends? The world?'

He nodded. 'Yes.'

Isla didn't know what to say! She had dreaded leaving. But she worried that they'd started this relationship weirdly. They'd moved in with one another, without dating, without getting to know one another. Would it cause ructions later on? That they'd missed steps?

'Isla... I never thought I could love another woman after Ellis... You've proved me wrong.'

Her own heart filled with a rush of happiness then. For him to say this, after all he'd been through with his wife. Her feelings for him were just as strong, but they'd not tested one another yet. Not fully. She had not been physical with him at all. They'd only kissed.

But he'd told her he loved her and she loved him and that required a celebration.

She leaned in for a kiss. A slow kiss. A passionate kiss. With the kiss she wanted to tell him everything. Wanted to show him how much he meant to her. To let him know that her feelings for him ran just as strong. Just as deep.

And as the kiss deepened he pushed her back against the wardrobe and she gasped with delicious heat that washed over her.

His hands, which before now had never strayed far from her hair, or neck, or waist, began to move up her body, and for the first time she felt his hands at her breasts, his thumbs brushing over her nipples, through her bathrobe, and the pressure of his desire against her.

Sex. He wanted sex.

And though she wanted more than anything in the world to be able to lie with him, already she could feel her panic building. She felt trapped. Claustrophobic. In a situation of her own making that she needed to escape from. She was just in her robe! She was vulnerable. He could have her naked in seconds! She got flashbacks of her attack, remembered the feel of that man's fumbling hands at her clothes, the way he'd tried to grab her, tried to get more and, suddenly, Isla was panicking and pushing Gabe away. 'Stop!'

He stepped back, eyes glazed with desire and guilt. 'I'm sorry. I didn't mean to—'

Isla suddenly felt cold. Afraid. What had she done? She wasn't ready for this! How had she ever thought she would be ready for this? 'No, I—'

There was a knock at her door and then Bea was coming in. 'Should I take this with me, do you think? I want to lend it to Harriet.' She was holding a book she'd bought and seemed totally oblivious to the tension in the room.

'Er…sure. Why not? Let's let Isla get dressed, so we can go,' Gabe said, ushering his daughter from the room.

Clearly he felt embarrassed, but so did she! How could she have feelings for him and practically tell him that she loved him, but would not be able to be with him *physically*? She couldn't play with his emotions like that—hadn't *he* been through enough? Hadn't they *both* been through enough?

This will never work. I can't believe I could ever be ready!

And how could she face him now? Clearly he couldn't face her. Her rejection, pushing him away, had upset him—he couldn't wait to escape!

Isla rubbed at her face as tears welled in her eyes. Would she ever get over this? Maybe those dreams of family were all pipe dreams. Maybe she'd been a fool to think that having feelings for someone would be enough to overcome the past.

She glanced at her jeans and sweater, then back at the wardrobe, and she knew she couldn't stay.

The drive to Hardwicke was difficult. Isla had not answered him when he'd knocked at her door to say they were ready to go and it had hurt him that she couldn't speak to him. Figuring it might be easier to talk when Bea wasn't around, he'd made a decision. 'I'll take Bea into school, then when I get back, we should talk,' he'd said quietly to her closed door.

She hadn't answered, but he'd known she was in there, listening.

He'd laid his forehead against the door. He

hadn't wanted to leave to take Bea to Hardwicke. He'd wanted to stay there. He'd wanted to sort this out. He'd felt awful! He'd asked for too much before she was ready. But he hadn't been able to help himself. She'd told him she felt the same way about him, they'd had a lovely day together and he'd missed being able to touch her and had wanted more and when they'd begun kissing... it had become so passionate, he'd craved more of her. Simple as that. He'd lost his senses as his need for her had grown. Forgetting he'd needed to go slowly. And now he was taking his daughter away, losing her, as well as walking away from Isla. He didn't want to lose her.

'Everything all right?' Bea asked in the car. Their journey had been completed in silence, because his mind was awash with regret and things he should have said. Should have done.

'Fine.'

'You don't look fine. You look sad.'

He glanced at Bea. Saw the concern on her face. 'I think I might have ruined Isla's birthday.'

'What did you do?'

How could he explain that to his daughter? She was twelve years old! 'I made a silly mistake, that's all, and it upset Isla.'

'Was it when I came into her room with my book?'

'You noticed that?'

'Anybody would have noticed that.'

'It's okay. Don't you worry about it. I'll sort it out when I get home. Apologise.'

'Make sure you do it properly. Mr Sansom says an apology should have three parts.'

'Really?' He couldn't believe he was taking romantic advice from his young daughter.

'Yes. We had this big class debate after Shawna fell out with Roland and everyone took sides.'

'Whose side did you take?'

'Shawna's.'

He pulled into the driveway of Hardwicke. 'And what are the three parts of an apology?' He figured right now that any advice would help, because he sure felt stuck about it all on his own.

'Hmm, let me remember… Oh, okay, I've got it. First of all you have to admit that the other person is upset about something and say you are sorry, but Mr Sansom says you really have to sound like you mean it.'

Gabe nodded. He could do that.

'Then, I think you have to admit that you did something wrong and work out how to put it right.'

'Okay, and the third part?'

'Make it better. Take the steps to actually make it right.'

'What did Shawna and Roland decide on?'

'She promised that she wouldn't put glue on his chair any more if he stopped calling her names.'

Gabe nodded, but he really wasn't worrying about Shawna or Roland. He figured those two were fine. What he needed to do was apologise to Isla for asking for more than she was ready to give. No. For trying to take more than what she was ready to give. He needed to accept his part. Show her that he knew what he had done wrong and the steps he would take to fix it. 'How did you get so wise?' he asked, leaning over to peck Bea on the cheek.

'I stayed here at Hardwicke.' She smiled at him, then the smile faltered. 'Will Isla still be your girlfriend when I get back next week?'

Gabe paused for a moment. 'I hope so. I hope so with all my heart.'

Isla felt an utter coward. She hadn't wanted to be there when Gabe got back from driving Bea to Hardwicke and so the second they'd gone down to the car park, she'd called a taxi and returned to her friend's flat. There'd been no photographers, so that was something. Maybe someone else was more interesting than she was, and she was glad. Because her life had enough misery in it—she hadn't wanted to have to fight her way to her front door.

The flat felt cold. She rubbed at her arms but

wasn't convinced the cold was from the flat. It was inside her. The flat was stale and so she opened up the windows to let in some fresh air. A thin layer of dust was on the shelves and, normally, she would have taken care of it, but right now? She didn't care. She slumped on the couch, seeing, but not hearing the drone of the television, lost in her turmoil of thoughts.

This place did not feel like home. Home had been where she was earlier today. A place where she had felt safe and cherished and loved. This place? Was a stopgap, nothing more, and honestly? She didn't want to be here. Maybe she could have taken a walk someplace? But you needed your wits about you in London and she knew right now that if she went out and about she wouldn't be concentrating. Just lost. She wiped her eyes and sniffed, feeling an utter failure. Gabe would never get to see the Isla she was before her life had changed for ever and that made her feel sad. That she couldn't be who she wanted to be.

A man like him deserved a woman who could love him back the way he needed. He was a red-blooded male, strong and passionate. He was *not* going to want to live the life of a monk!

A knock at her door startled her from her reverie.

Who was it? Who even knew she was back? Could it be Gabe?

Her heart pounded at the possibility and she glanced at the clock on the wall. Had there been enough time for him to, not only go to Hardwicke and back, but also find her gone and make the only logical conclusion as to her whereabouts?

The answer was yes.

She got up and went to the door. Curious as to who was waiting outside. She peered through the eyehole and saw Gabe on the other side. Because of the distortion, she couldn't see if he was mad or sad or anything at all. 'What do you want?' she asked through the door, her heart breaking.

'Only to speak with you. Preferably face to face, but I can do this through a door, if you want the rest of the people in this block to hear me,' he said, sounding calm and friendly.

And he was right. They'd already had enough of their relationship put into the public eye. Maybe some of it, especially this most important part, should remain private? Isla pulled back the chain and opened the door, stepping back.

'Come in.' She was not afraid of him. She had no misconceptions about whether he'd be angry or mad with her, because she knew him well. He'd just want to talk. That was all.

He followed her into the small living room.

'It's not your place, but it's home,' she said, attempting a joke.

'Is it, though?'

She looked up at him.

Gabe shook his head. 'May I sit down?'

She indicated a chair and sat opposite.

'I'm here to apologise. I'd like you to hear me out and if, at the end, we can't agree on a way forward, then by all means I shall leave you in peace and see you at work tomorrow, but I really hope that you'll want to hear me out.'

Isla nodded. She wanted to hear what he had to say. Just to be near him again was wonderful and she'd hated the short time they'd been apart, thinking that it might all be over.

'I'm sorry for what happened before. I'm sorry if I upset you, or made you feel scared. Frightened by my unthinking actions. I was wrong to push for more before you were ready. I should have gone more slowly. Waited for you to guide me as to when you were ready for more physical contact and awaited your consent on that. I was wrong and I hate that I've upset you, or scared you, or made you think of what happened to you from before. That was not and will never be my intention and, if you'll permit me, I'd like to make amends. Show you that I can move at your pace and will be guided by you in the future.'

'You think we have a future?' she asked, terrified.

'I do.' He smiled. 'An incredible one! We're good together, Isla! At least, I think so! I never thought I could love someone again and yet here I am. I love you and I want to be with you in any way that you can manage to be. I can go slow. I can wait for you to be ready, and if it's the case that you'll never be ready? Well, then, that's perfectly fine, too. But I would like you to be a significant part in my life. In Bea's life, too. And I would love for you to come home, so we can begin that life.'

Isla almost couldn't believe it! He was saying all these wonderful things! 'I want to be ready. I want to work towards being ready. Maybe I need some more therapy.' She laughed nervously. 'But I would like to be with you very much. Are you sure you can wait for me? I don't want to punish you by holding you at arm's length. Not when I love you with all of my heart, too.'

Gabe smiled. 'You do?'

'Of course I do!'

He got up. Came over to sit beside her. Gently took her hands in his. 'We can do this, you know.'

She nodded. 'I'm sorry I ran.'

'I'm sorry I pushed.'

'You think we'll ever get to be where we'd both like to be?'

He smiled. 'I'm *already* there.'

She wanted to kiss him. 'Then let's go home.'

EPILOGUE

One year and one day later

SHE SLIPPED FROM his arms and crept across the bedroom floor, trying not to make a noise. She didn't want to wake Gabe. Neither of them had got much sleep and now that he was sleeping, she wanted him to get some rest.

Yesterday had been her birthday and, unlike her birthday from the previous year, where Gabe had treated her, she'd decided to give him a present.

They'd been intimate before, of course. It had taken about eight months before she'd felt ready to go all the way with him, and it had been everything she'd ever dreamed it would be. She'd been a little nervous! Like, what if, after all of this, they weren't sexually compatible? But that idea had been blown away in an instant. Gabe's very touch had been enough to make every sensory nerve ending in her body sing. He'd been gentle. Delicate. Moving slowly. Taking his time.

Savouring every inch of her, the way she'd felt she could savour him. She'd not wanted to be passive. She'd wanted to take what she wanted, too, and his groans of pleasure as she'd teased and tempted him had filled her with a sense of her own feminine power and control.

The realisation that making love with Gabe no longer had to be something that she feared had been inexplicably powerful. That it was something that she'd be able to enjoy had been a wonderful surprise.

They'd taken small steps in the lead-up to it. Isla had employed a therapist, who'd suggested they take the notion of sex away completely and instead just do small things. Little, intimate things. A touch here. A stroke there. A kiss. A lick. And if she didn't want to go any further, then she didn't have to. In fact, the therapist had forbidden it.

Which had made her want it all the more.

Her sexual homework had become something that Isla had begun to look forward to as each week passed and holding back had become something with which they'd both struggled. One week, the therapist had suggested that Gabe do nothing but just lie there and let Isla do what she wanted to do. He wasn't to hold her, or guide her, and, basically, just lie back and think of England!

Isla had wanted to throw caution to the wind and go further, but Gabe had been the one to remind her that they shouldn't.

She'd been a little upset at that. Feared that he didn't want her. But he'd shown her differently by going over and over the last step they'd been allowed. It had involved him using his tongue in a very particular way and she'd welcomed it. Over and over again as she'd revelled in her power and her femininity and realised that she could guide this, too. She wasn't weaker than him. She wasn't submissive. Gabe's physical touch, their lovemaking, could be something that gave her power and control and it was all that they had needed.

And the week when the therapist had told them that they could engage in full lovemaking if she felt that she was ready? Isla had come home, grabbed Gabe's hand and pulled *him* up the stairs!

She smiled at the thought of it. At all the nights they'd had together since then. She and Gabe had built something beautiful, something wondrous, and she was so thrilled with her life. With her love for Gabe and Bea.

She closed the door to the en suite quietly and crept to the cupboard where she'd hidden the box. Isla had always wanted to create her own family and they'd had genetic counselling, too, due to

Bea's cystic fibrosis. And so they'd spent many nights enjoying each other. Almost as if they were trying to play catch up with all the nights they'd spent at each other's side without being allowed to go all the way.

Her period was a couple of days late. Not much and it was probably nothing, but she'd wanted this so much and for so long, she simply had to know the truth.

If the test was negative, then that would be disappointing, but it would also be fine. They'd not been doing this all that long and they still had all the time in the world to get pregnant. She would be sad, but it would pass, because she still had the love of her life. And she had a wonderful stepdaughter in Bea. Not officially her stepdaughter, not yet. They weren't married. But that was how she felt about Bea. She loved her too.

To be able to give Bea and Gabe this gift of a sibling? Another child? After all their struggles? After all that they'd both been through? It would be amazing.

And secretly, selfishly, just for herself, she yearned to have a baby. Gabe had already experienced that with Ellis, but Isla never had. She'd never ever had a scare, or anything. She'd never come close. But now she was and she wanted this more than anything.

She took the test and placed the stick on the side beside the sink and waited. There was a full-length mirror in the en suite and she looked at herself. Front view. Side view, running a hand over her belly, imagining it swelling and filling with child. She thought she felt a little different, but maybe that was just her imagination? Maybe that was just being overly hopeful? But she'd been tired lately.

And yesterday? On her birthday? It had been a long day of celebration and she'd wanted to be in bed early. They'd gone to bed at eight p.m. Lain in each other's arms and laughed about the day. She'd turned to face him. Had entwined her naked body with his and looked deeply into his eyes as her hands had begun to explore. She'd not been tired enough for that. Now that she could, she wanted to enjoy intimacy as much as she could with Gabe.

He was perfect. He was her everything. And if this test was negative? He still would be. If it was positive? Then he'd still be her everything, but somehow so much more. She wanted his child in her belly. She wanted to grow their family. Her ultimate power as a woman.

Was it time? How many minutes had elapsed? Enough? What if she looked and it was still too early? But she couldn't wait any longer. She'd waited enough.

Isla crept over to the stick, closed her eyes and sucked in a steadying breath, before opening them again and looking down.

Pregnant

She gasped, her heart pounding and expanding with joy as she studied it closer just to make sure.

She heard Gabe stir in the next room and knew she'd have no way to keep this from him, to plan a surprise way of telling him, because she wanted him to share in her joy, to share in this precious moment that she would remember for the rest of her life. 'Gabe? You awake?'

'Yes.'

'Can you come in here a minute?'

There was a pause and she imagined him creeping across the bedroom floor, naked, grabbing his robe maybe?

'Everything okay?' he asked, opening the door.

She turned to him. 'I hope so.' And she lifted the test and watched as his smile broke across his face.

'We're having a baby?'

She nodded and laughed as he picked her up and spun her round in his arms.

'My God, how I love you! You've made my life, my heart, so happy.'

'Well, I hope there's room for more love in that heart,' she said, smiling.

'Are you kidding me? Of course there is. You

make it possible.' He dropped to his knees, rested his hands on her belly, cradling it, and kissed it. 'Welcome to the world, little one.'

* * * * *

If you enjoyed this story,
check out these other great reads from
Louisa Heaton

A Mistletoe Marriage Reunion
Finding Forever with the Firefighter
Single Mom's Alaskan Adventure
Bound by Their Pregnancy Surprise

All available now!

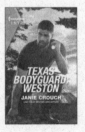